LEXI

AND THE MAGIC CATS

An Extraordinary Tale ...

Roxanne J. Barker

Lexi and the Magic Cats

An Extraordinary Tale

Copyright 2022—by Roxanne J. Barker

First Edition—May 2022

Published—DTP Impressions

Cover—DC Cover

Creations Artwork—Roxanne J. Barker

Developmental Editor—Alorah Arliotis

Copy Editor—Keryn Delaney

Typesetting—Rose Elphick, DTP Impressions

ISBN: 978-1-3999-1250-1

'Inside us all is a sense of wonderment'

TABLE OF CONTENTS

Chapters:

Dedicated to Aunt Jean and Uncle Eric Stuart.

With love

CHAPTER 1
The Adventure Begins

I FELT A BURST of excitement whoosh right through me. I took in a huge gulp, a goldfish-size bubble of air, and held it. This was my first ever flight.

I was sitting in a ginormous aeroplane about to take off from London Heathrow.[1] My eyes shut tight, as tight as could be. My fingers gripped the seat and locked. A rush of air exhaled from my cheeks, forcing my lungs to sink inwards. I was both excited and scared.

The engines roared, accelerating to top speed. We were travelling super-fast along the runway, then lifted. Up! Up! Up, way up, into the sky above the clouds. I went as pale as one could ever imagine—ghostly pale.

'You look as if you've seen a ghost, Lexi.' Mum's warm hand gently covered mine.

'I'm oh-oh-ok, Mum,' I struggled to get my words out.

The loud roar quietened down to a purring, humming sound. Slowly I turned my head, stretching my neck ever-so-slightly to peer out of the small, round cabin window.

'Look...' I said. 'All the pretty lights.'

Fiddlelights! [2]

Beneath me was a vast universe covered in twinkles and sparkles. Below, London changed into a miniature, magical toy town. Tiny car headlights were shining on narrow little streets.

'It's just like Fairyland!' I whispered under my breath, relieved we hadn't crashed down to earth. Daylight was beginning to fade. The pink and grey, dusky night sky began to show itself.

'The colour in your cheeks is coming back, darling. Are you feeling better?' Mum asked, lifting a strand of hair off my face.

'Yes, Mum,' I replied, following a big, pretend smile. I was already missing Prushka, my pedigree blue-grey cat, who comforts me when I feel shy, unhappy, or uncomfortable.

Smiling is my way of hiding my feelings. I practice over and over, looking into a mirror—my wide mouth, showy teeth, and big eyes create a big happy, pretend smile. It works every time. No one else knows I struggle with shyness, except for me. Well, that's what I hoped.

It was the February school holidays. Mum had decided to take me on my first winter holiday in Germany to see the snow and visit cousin Ellette and her friend, Gustav.

Ellette had been born in The Forest and still lives in the same dwelling, far away from anyone, except for one neighbour, Granddad Edric. He lives with Master Horatio, his mysterious wise owl, and Tobias, his mischievous pig.

Mum and her niece Ellette made a promise. They secretly arranged an extraordinary adventure for me. I stared at my Mum lovingly. She looked so pretty in her blue dress. I felt proud that she was my Mum.

'Oh, I forgot to mention that you'll be meeting the most extraordinary cats. I'm not sure if you will find them as friendly as Prushka, but you will find them…how do I say this…unusual.' Mum yawned widely, dozing off. I wondered what she meant by "unusual".

'Tea, coffee, juice, water, young lady?' The unexpected voice startled me. My eyes darted upwards towards the voice, my ears alert. The Flight Attendant serving drinks smiled at me kindly. I always feel silly when grown-ups speak to me. I want to hide somewhere, anywhere.

Fiddlevanish!

I wished and wished my shyness could disappear forever and ever. It made me angry with myself. I wanted to achieve top grades in drama class. I was in year six at school, ten years old, and already knew I wanted to create magical films when I was older.

I tugged on Mum's sleeve.

'Pardon, Miss?' The Flight Attendant looked down at me and then at my Mum. She waited patiently.

Holding up one perfectly manicured hand, Mum pointed in my direction and spoke for me. 'She'll have tea, a sprinkle of sugar and err… almond milk if you have it please?'

'My daughter is very shy,' explained Mum. The Flight Attendant smiled politely.

'That's perfectly fine,' she gazed fixedly at me.

I ignored what Mum said about my shyness and changed the subject. I know Mum is concerned about my extreme shyness and hopes that I will simply grow out of it. Little does she know that pointing out my shyness makes me feel more awkward.

'Is she from Thunderbirds?'[3] I whispered, leaning in towards Mum when the pretty attendant had gone. Mum took another look at her. 'She might be. Those uniforms are similar.' Mum gently squeezed my hand.

'I'm feeling better, Mum.'

Please fasten your seat belts. A sign lit up over our heads.

'We're landing, Lexi,' Mum said, frantically flicking crumbs off her lap.

A sudden rush of excitement jolted me to sit upright. It startled me. There was a shuddering, knocking, sound coming from underneath us. Mum explained the airplane wheels were being released, ready to land.

Double-checking my seat belt was on securely, I clasped my hands together tightly as the plane started to descend for landing.

'Now, where's my handbag? Can you see it?' Mum said, stretching over me.

'Under your chair, look. No, there.' I waved a finger in the direction. I knew perfectly well what was coming. *Mega embarrassing.*

'Here we go,' I mumbled, rolling my eyes as I watched the zip of her handbag slide open from one side to the other. Her hand disappeared into the bag, dipping into the unknown. First up: came her make-up mirror. Mum's lips began shaping into a round 'O'. Her lips pouted, waiting for the gooey pink stuff to spread all over them.

Second up: her favourite fluffy powder puff. It had a life of its own, sprinkling powder all over her nose. I glared.

'To cover my shiny nose darling,' said mum.

I had heard those exact words before. She took one last look in her mirror from left to right. Satisfied, she plopped her make-up brushes, puffs, and lipsticks back into her expensive designer handbag.

'That's better. I can face the world now.' Mum let out a happy sigh.

Then turning back to me: 'Can you *what* darling, you were going to ask something?' Her one eyebrow raised itself.

'Nothing…' my voice dragged.

'You sure? I know you're upset when your eyes roll,' she replied questioningly.

'Yes.' I said abruptly, annoyed with myself. When I really, really want to ask for something, I don't.

Fiddlegrump!

The plane approached the ground with a gentle pull on the powerful brakes. I could see the runway out of the window.

Chatter started up inside our cabin, raising the noise and energy levels as everyone waited eagerly to exit.

'Ladies and Gentlemen welcome to Frankfurt airport.[4]'

'Meine Damen und Herren willkommen auf den Frankfurter Flughafen.'

Tired but happy, we packed our luggage into the boot of the sleek, silver hire car and drove towards the motorway.

'There's no speed limit on the autobahn[5], Lexi. Cars go as fast as they like,' Mum shouted above the whirring noise.

'Autoba...?' I had to raise my voice, too.

'A..U..T..O..B..A..H..N.' Mum spelt it out.

'One neeaow—two neeaow—three neeaow—four neeaow—five—' The cars raced along autobahn. Awesome!

'What are you doing, darling?'

'Counting how many cars pass us.' I replied. I wanted Mum to speed up.

We were driving on the opposite side of the road to what we are accustomed to. It felt odd. I watched the land whizz by— everything out there was skimming along super-fast.

I pretended I was in a low, flying saucer, inspecting the earth. We drove and drove for miles and miles. It seemed to go on forever.

It was getting darker. Oh wait…maybe.

'At last. There's a sign for the Nature Park. We must be close.' Mum gave a sigh of relief and turned the car at the signpost.

She drove into The Forest, and soon we were surrounded by giant trees. It felt *eerie*. We were in total darkness, apart from the powerful headlights of the car. It was the only car on a long, dark, sandy road.

I looked up at the bright moonlight flooding The Forest and fields around us. We were cocooned in a mysterious land. I felt an electrical shudder go down my spine. I shivered. The hairs on the back of my neck stood on end. I had a strange sensation of a Ghostly Being tickling me with a long, crooked finger.

'I'm getting goosebumps,' I yelped.

A musty smell suddenly caught my attention.

'Mum can you smell…?'

'Oh, yes. Where's it coming from?' Mum's nose crinkled upwards and then smoothed down again.

'Maybe from the fields?'

'Yes, maybe,' I replied, and as quickly as I had answered it had disappeared.

'It's getting very late, Lexi. I'm tired and can't go much further.' Mum yawned.

'Let's check into the hotel where we are staying, have a good night's sleep, and find Ellette's cabin in the morning.'

'I'll send Ellette a voice message.'

I pouted. I wanted to see my cousin now.

A short drive off the main road took us to a small, quaint hotel in the local village. It had a magical air about it and looked ancient. Standing proudly on the front lawn was a giant, blue ceramic rooster.

'What's the red thing on his head called?' I asked curiously.

'That's the cockscomb, and those fleshy flaps underneath his chin, on his throat, are known as a wattle.'

'Those are funny words.'

The owners of the small country hotel spoke perfect English and welcomed us warmly. They are Ellette's friends.

We enjoyed a simple supper of toast, boiled eggs, and tea, in our spacious room. I felt happy at the Blue Rooster Hotel. The big, blue rooster with his bright red cockscomb stood on the front lawn guarding us all night.

'Is that your tummy making that noise?' Mum asked.

'Yes.' I replied sheepishly.

We set off to find Ellette as my tummy continued its relentless gurgle. I hadn't eaten my breakfast. Everything was very different. I felt overly excited and shy in the dining room.

I longed for a slice of yummy chocolate fudge cake, with icing on top. My thoughts ran wild as I imagined every delicious mouthful with its creamy, fudgy filling. It was my favourite cake.

'I would love a slice of chocolate cake, please.' My mind flooded with the thought and *smell* of cake.

'I have some dark chocolate in my bag.'

'Err, I *don't like* dark chocolate, Mum.'

'I know, darling, but it is chocolate.'

Fiddlechoc!

We drove on a little further, searching for a small, bright blue letterbox, numbered 14a, hidden amongst tall trees. 'First one to spot the letterbox, gets a prize,' Mum sang in a high shrill voice.

'Is that it?' I pointed to a letterbox nestled between two tall Fir trees, just visible in the distance.

'I win! I win! What's the prize, Mum? Oh! I know. Cake, cake and more cake. Please, please,' I pleaded.

'Yes! You win,' Mum answered, keeping her eyes on the road.

'This must be it, Lexi,' cheered Mum, ignoring my sulky face. I wanted the cake now.

Ellette had left the green metal gate open for our arrival. We drove onto the property, and suddenly cake was forgotten. I felt safe and calm.

We were surrounded by complete stillness. The only sound was the car tyres rolling over the gravel, down the muddy track.

The long, winding lane twisted ahead of us, then disappeared into the distance.

My mood changed as I took in deep, pine-scented breaths. The magnificent trees stood tall and proud. Holding out wide, furry gentle giant arms. Their dark green, needle-like leaves beckoned us like a thousand fingers, encouraging us to enter their world. I felt tingly and happy to be alive.

I stared out of the car window and gasped at the snow-covered surroundings. Just then, magically, an opening appeared directly in front of us. The rays of the bright golden sun blinded me for a moment as they shone piercingly through the car windscreen.

'Your sunglasses, Lexi, please,' said Mum, rummaging through her handbag with one hand as I shielded my eyes from the glare. I didn't want to put them on, but the sun was ever so bright. I feel self-conscious when Mum tells me to wear sunglasses.

Fiddleblush!

Slowly, Mum drove down the tree-lined driveway and pulled the car up, outside a huge, rambling, log cabin. It had an air of mystery hovering over it. Perhaps the magic and mystery spread throughout The Forest that stretched around the cabin for miles.

The old wooden cabin was nestled amongst a snow-covered Alpine Forest in the middle of nowhere. The entire region was filled with charm and magic.

I leapt out of the car. I wanted to explore immediately.

Next to the parking area stood a tall greenhouse, the walls and windows, frosted glass. I walked up to the large double sliding doors, stood on tip-toes, peered inside, not sure what I might see.

I also noticed a well-hidden wooden shelter with a bright purple caravan parked beneath it. I couldn't believe my eyes. Oh! What fun.

Everything I saw around me set my imagination alight. Magic was definitely afoot. It would be easy to feel disorientated. Was the landscape altering ever so slightly?

Alongside the purple caravan, on a make-shift wooden porch, stood an old blue sofa, and leaning up against it, was a genuine witch's broomstick[6].

'Mum, look at this!' I said, waving my arms in the air excitedly. 'Does a witch live in there?'

'Lexi, button up your coat, and let's find Ellette. You can explore later.'

Mum walked towards the wooden cabin, which had a lopsided chimney.

I felt a surge of excitement that fizzed and popped, all the way down to my toes. Wow!

Hmmm… there were definitely hidden secrets here. I had stepped into a world full of enchantment and wonder. If the broom could talk, I'm sure it would have many tales to tell.

A small cottage beyond Ellette's sprawling wooden cabin looked intriguing. I skipped towards it and discovered what looked like a fairy-ring drawing I'd seen in one of my books in the middle of a grassy area. The circular pattern was clearly marked in the soft, green grass.

A wooden bird-table stood right in the centre of the ring. I felt a warm glow come over me. My body began to shake ever so slightly. What was happening? I felt like I could *burst* with excitement.

'Wait for me!' I called, running after Mum. She waited patiently for me at the front door before knocking. Moments later, Ellette flung open the door with a massive surge of energy and spontaneously hugged my Mum.

'Hello, Kitty, darling Aunt!' Ellette expressed with glee.

'You're looking very well, Ellette. Did you enjoy your birthday? How old are you now? The Forest air is kind to you,' Mum responded with equal warmth and excitement.

'I'm as young as I choose.' She giggled and twinkled.

Ellette's voice filled me with joy. She stood on tip-toes, both arms stretched wide, and gathered me in her embrace. Her joyful laughter rang in my ears.

'Hello, my darling Lexi. My, you're getting tall.' She kissed me on both cheeks then hugged me tightly. I could smell the fragrance of flowers wafting elegantly around me.

'Ellette, you are truly beautiful.' I whispered.

Her blue-green velvet dress, with wild-swirling patterns, was astonishingly magical. As if she had danced off the pages of a fairytale book. I had forgotten how snow-white her hair was, yet she looked so young, with her fine porcelain features and cherry red lips. A gracious, elfin Princess with dancing blue eyes stood before me.

Standing some distance behind her was her friend, Gustav.

Tall, lean, with dark wispy hair and strangely pointed features. He didn't join in at first but stood a few steps away from us, observing, with a gentle smile on his face. Gustav seemed reserved or shy. Like me, he didn't say much.

If grown-ups are shy, then it must be perfectly fine for me to be shy, too.

Surrounding the cabin stood a dense, snow-white forest. It stretched for miles. There was a strong, tingling energy coming from the trees, and the air felt crisp and alive.

I knew creatures could be watching every step, listening to every word. Tiny fairy lights flickered between spiky branches. I was sure I could hear whispers and even occasional giggles.

I knew this was a holiday I would never forget!

CHAPTER 2

Queeny

'BRRR...' ELLETTE RUBBED her arms briskly to warm up.

'Come on in, *es ist sehr kalt.*'

'*Darf ich ihre Mäntel nehmen?*' Gustav mimed, taking off his coat. We did the same. I felt unsure because I didn't understand his language. Mum handed her coat to Gustav and helped me with mine.

'*Danke schon.*'

'*Bitte schon.*'

Gustav was different. I couldn't help staring at him. He had deep-set bright blue-green eyes. His expressive eyebrows were jet black, as was his short, neat beard. By all accounts, Gustav was pretty as well as handsome.

His gentle energy and soft voice fascinated me. I was a natural at picking up people's energy, or 'vibes', so my school friends said. Gustav felt good and, oh, so very 'shiny'. I was entranced.

'Gustav speaks a little English,'
added Ellette. She translated as she and
Gustav spoke to one another, before she
disappeared into the room next door. Ellette
spoke English, German and several other
languages. I was impressed.

She reappeared, re-arranging her thick
hair after removing her hat.

'How's school, Ellette? Do you enjoy
teaching drama?' Mum asked.

'Yes! Good, thank you. We're doing very
well this term. I love my new job.'

'I must say, you look radiant in those
bright colours.'

'Thank you, Kitty.'

'Bright colours make me happy, and all my pupils love me wearing them.'

Moving towards the fireplace, Ellette said:

'Let's warm up by the fire.'

Tiny blue lights danced above her head. My eyes were transfixed as the sparkling lights seemed to twirl around her crown. Had anyone else noticed?

'How are you getting on in your drama classes, Lexi?' Ellette enquired.

'I'm not,' I replied, hiding behind Mum. I felt coy when Ellette spoke to me directly. My cheeks flushed, but I didn't want her to notice how shy I was.

'She dreams of being an actor, one day.' Mum smiled, reaching for my hand.

Oh no! My cheeks were glowing even brighter.

'No, Mum,' I paused. 'I want to be a *filmmaker*.' I swiftly squished tears of frustration as I closed my eyes, wiping the telltale wetness away.

'I am sure this holiday will be wonderful for you, Lexi. You'll go back home, a new person,' announced Ellette jubilantly.

We followed her into a circular-shaped room. A strong woody scent flooded the air, making me splutter and cough. Suddenly,

I felt giddy. A tickle in my throat made me cough even more.

Vintage books stood in messy rows along shelves on a giant tree-shaped bookcase. On one side of the room, hanging on a long clothes rail, were vividly coloured fabrics made up of tops, tutus, dresses, coats, and various other costumes in every colour of the rainbow. What were they *for*? I was fascinated.

'Do you still play the flute, Ellette? I see a case over there in the corner,' Mum asked.

'Only now and again. I've been rushed off my feet recently, getting ready for the school play,' Ellette explained.

I wished she was the drama teacher at my school. I had already decided that she was the kindest, most caring person in the entire world. It radiated from her! I wanted to tell her, but I couldn't get the words out.

'Come through,' Ellette gestured towards the kitchen.

Without warning, a strange smell in the kitchen hit my nose. What was that awful smell? *Sniff... sniff... sniffle...*

My tummy turned. I felt like I might throw up.

'Uh, uh, oh... no...' I couldn't speak.

Thanks to her sensitive sense of smell, my mum's nostrils were also twitching, but she

29

didn't comment. I giggled to myself playfully.

Fiddlepong!

The adults gathered around a large, wood-burning stove, which stood old but proud, in the centre of the room. I moved towards the cosy, hot stove, hands outstretched.

'No! Don't touch that, Lexi,' Ellette cried out and dashed forward, grabbing my hands. 'It's boiling hot,' she frowned at me, then burst into joyful laughter as soon as she knew I was out of harm's way.

'Sit over here,' Ellette coaxed me across the room while she plumped up a huge, soft feather cushion.

I couldn't speak. I felt silly and ever so shy. We eventually gathered at a round, wooden table and sat on rickety old chairs.

I was seated next to a large picture window. From where I sat, the view of The Forest was mesmerising. I felt all snuggly inside the cabin. It looked bitterly cold and other-worldly outside.

I stared out of the window at the mystical winter scene to distract myself from the pungent odour coming from the kitchen. Finally, I began to relax a little.

'Did you say there will be snow again tomorrow, Ellette?'

'Yes Kitty, definitely,' Ellette replied.

Gustav was standing at the kitchen sink, wearing bright yellow gloves, too big for his hands. He turned the taps with all his strength and waited patiently while clutching a bright red kettle.

Suddenly the water spluttered, then gushed through the old pipes with a SHUDDER, a BANG, a WALLOP, and a loud SQUEEEAAAKKK. It splashed forcefully into the kettle.

'The water is coming through!' Ellette joyfully clapped her delicate hands together.

'Wonderful, *wunderbar*,' she sang. Her energy lit up the whole kitchen. Again, tiny flashes of blue light appeared around her head. Ever so curious! Was I imagining them?

There was definitely something different about Gustav. I couldn't quite work it out. Not yet... *I really liked his vibe.*

'Are you ready to eat, everyvun?' Gustav asked politely.

I was starving. Gustav had cooked baked potatoes, topped with melted gooey, (stinky), stretchy cheese. Could the cheese possibly be the strange whiff in the house? I cautiously sniffed at the cheese. Hmmm, it *was*.

I was too shy to say that the smell of the cheese was gross, so I started with a cautious nibble, only to discover it was actually delicious.

After we had all filled our bellies, tea was served.

'Gustav, this tea? What is it?' Mum asked rather abruptly, her cheeks puckering up.

'It is mixed herbs from ze forest,' he replied, somewhat puzzled by Mum's tone. He rubbed his beard anxiously.

My taste buds quivered. It wasn't that I *couldn't* drink the tea, but it tasted like bitter witch's brew, made from stinky herbs and mouse droppings. It was the weirdest tea ever!

Fiddleyuck!

I desperately wanted chocolate fudge cake with my tea. I felt disappointed when I realised there was no cake on offer. Could I be *bold* and ask Ellette if she had any cake?

Fiddlefudge!'

I caught sight of small luminous stickers, in the shape of stars, five stuck to the kitchen glass window.

'Why are there stars on the window, Ellette?' I touched them gently with my fingertips.

'They're Star-Lights for the fairies,'
she whispered. A larger, twinkly light
miraculously appeared just behind her head.
The Star-Light sparkled intensely, with the
ceiling light shining down on us, but quickly
disappeared. As it did, Ellette pulled me into
her arms and hugged me.

She found my hand and put a small, clear,
crystal[7] into my palm.

'The magic has begun,' she whispered,
'shhh....' she gestured, placing her index
finger to her lips, 'it's our secret.'

I sneaked a peek at the warm pulsing
crystal. Inside that crystal was a star-shaped
crystal, and *another*, and *another*, and another!
Ellette whispered that is was a Phantom
Crystal[8].

FAIRIES! Real Fairies.

Ok! The word fairies had my attention. I
pressed my nose against the windowpane.
My eyes were wide open, trying not to blink.
I stood at the kitchen window holding my
magnificent crystal, waiting for the fairies.

I scanned The Forest, searching for fairies
behind every tree. I inspected every branch
and leaf. I waited and waited for a Fairy
Being to appear.

'Come on, fairies, show yourselves,' I
implored, 'I know you're out there.'

I was determined to see them. I hoped with all my heart that a fairy would appear at the window and tap on the glass.

'*Pleeeeease, come,*' I sighed and dreamily wandered back to the table, the crystal hidden safely in my pocket. I could feel it pulsing—vrrrh, vrrrh, vrrrh—against my leg.

Without warning, there was a loud *BANG*. It brought me back to reality. I felt a soft, furry creature rubbing against my legs from under the wooden table. Cautiously, I hung upside down, peering beneath the table.

Two large, bright, golden eyes met the tip of my nose. The huge cat and I eyeballed each other. I stared, wide-eyed and open-mouthed in sheer amazement. Wow! This golden-brown tabby cat was truly magnificent.

In a flash, she hurled herself through a unique cat-flap under the table. The big cat proudly landed at my feet.

'PURR-NEOW…' she said, peering directly at me with great curiosity.

'Lexi, meet Queeny.' Ellette giggled.

'MEEOW… MEEOW.' Queeny responded joyfully, pleased to be the centre of attention.

Ellette bent down and swooped the enormous ball of golden-brown fluff into her arms.

I noticed queeny had extra-long, whiskers and piercing golden-yellow eyes. Her majestic presence took my breath away.

Fiddlewow!

'My beautiful magical Queeny. Kisses and more kisses,' Ellette sang in a high-pitched voice.

'PURRR… MEOW… PRR… PRR…
PRRR…,' Queeny replied.

Ellette continued to fuss Queeny, rubbing
her under her chin. I looked on, fascinated by
this remarkable cat.

I crawled under the table to study
Gustav's handiwork. It was the biggest
cat-flap I had ever seen.

'That's massive.'

'Gustav built it for Queeny, because she is
clearly my largest cat,' Ellette chuckled.

She rubbed Queeny on the head, speaking
in a mysterious voice. A cat-language of
their own?

'Queeny, weeny, precious Queeny…'

'How many cats do you have, Ellette?' I
asked after recovering from the surprise and
finally finding my voice.

'We have four cats. Actually, it's five
altogether,' she replied as she smiled at
Queeny, rhythmically circling her elegant
fingers round her treasured cat's ears.

Queeny seemed to be smiling back.

'May I meet all the cats, please?' I leaned
forward, cautiously touching Queeny's
golden brown fur. I wanted to ensure she
wouldn't scratch.

'Yes, of course.'

But when, I wondered.

This time I would be fully prepared for the next high-spirited cat that leapt through the giant cat-flap.

Queeny looked me straight in the eye. I sensed her mood changing—her ears were pointing straight up. Yikes!

'MEEAHOW!'

Her bottom wiggled furiously, and her tail began waving rapidly from side to side. She had a 'ready-to-pounce' facial expression as she focused her intense gaze on me. I froze, then I heard another very loud

'MEEAH-OW! PRR-NEEOWW...' Without a warning, Queeny took an almighty leap into the air. The magnificent furry mass flew towards me. Large paws and claws stretched out in front of her. With a considerable *OOMPH*—Queeny landed skillfully on my lap. Everyone in the room held their breath, startled and amused.

'Are you going to bite me or cuddle me?' I asked meekly.

'Oh! You're a heavy lump Queeny.'

I was rigid, afraid to move. I had been outsmarted by a cat. Queeny began purring, pushing and pressing as she kneaded her paws deep into my tummy and legs, over and over again.

PURRR... PURRR... PURRR-NEOW... she said.

Push... pull... push... her claws expanding and contracting as she massaged my body.

'*Ouch!*' I cried out, but I didn't move. I sat as still as I could, my eyes wide with interest and amusement

Once her comfort-kneading was complete, she poised for a while, then jumped onto the floor, turning her head to look me in the eye. She swaggered off with a spirited attitude. I loved her instantly. I just knew she was a super special cat.

'MEAW... MEEUW... MEEUW...', her loud voice continued as she trotted across the floor towards an oversized, plump floor cushion beside the stove.

Cleverly, she created a soft area with her paws, then, turning round and round in circles, she curled up and began preening her thick fur coat. The warmth of the hot stove and the busy grooming session had Queeny fast asleep in no time.

There was something wonderful, yet curiously strange, about dearest Queeny. It was as if *she knew me:* My thoughts, even my feelings. Queeny was a uniquely special cat, indeed. She had things to teach me. Of that, I was sure. What exactly had Mum meant when she said the cats were unusual? Hmmm...

CHAPTER 3
Hide and Seek

I THOUGHT OF Queeny the second I opened my eyes. I flung my covers aside, jumped out of bed, and pulled back the curtains. My heart leaped with joy seeing bright, white, glistening snow. It looked like glitter was covering the hotel grounds for as far as I could see.

'Mum! Mum! It's snowing. Come quickly.'

'It's snow-land. Look!' I did a round-about-spin on one leg, jumped, followed by a dive onto my bed. I was filled with *so much* excitement.

Mum was at the dressing table, brushing her hair. She walked over to the window.

'How beautiful, Lexi,' she said casually, then sat back down to apply her favourite pink lipstick. She sipped dainty mouthfuls of tea, leaving thick lipstick marks on the rim of the cup, then applied even *more* gooey lipstick. Ugh!

I stared out of the window with longing. I watched a group of children playing in the snow. Snowballs flew high in the air and crashed down, landing in soft, powdery mounds all around the snow-covered garden.

Oh, I wished I had friends to have fun with. My shyness always got in the way of making new friends. A deep sigh escaped from my chest.

'Oh well,' I whispered and stepped away from the window.

Fiddlefun!

I couldn't wait to get back to The Forest to explore. I dressed hurriedly, making sure I was warm enough. I tidied my shoulder-length, blonde hair and was ready to go. Yay!

On the way, Mum made a surprise detour, driving instead to an olde worlde village bakery.

My mouth watered as I entered the shop. My eyes expanded wide. The aroma of cakes, bread baking, and chocolate was delicious. A colourful display of sweet delights sat on top of the counter.

'They ALL look yummy.'

Behind the glass, a display of five mouth-watering chocolate cakes neatly placed next to each other caught my gaze. The shop-keeper spoke in English:

'Ve have Chocolate Chip, Chocolate Dip, Chocolate Cream, Chocolate Buttons and finally *ze best* CHOCOLATE FUDGE CAKE.'

'That one, PLEASE!' I pointed directly to the chocolate fudge cake. I smiled cheekily at the shopkeeper. I was in cake heaven. Oh, my! I was so excited. Finally. *Cake*!

The chocolate fudge cake was carefully wrapped and placed in a beautiful pink square box. I watched everything. Swirls of golden writing went on top, then trimmed with a silver ribbon and bows.

Something caught my eye as we left the bakery. A dinky shop was just across the street, decorated in green and white stripes. It was a proper candy store. Wow!

'Can we go in there?' I asked, raising my voice with enthusiasm.

'Another time, Lexi dear, Ellette and Gustav are waiting for us. I prefer to drive while there is no snow falling. It's easier to see the road.'

'Ugh!' I kicked at the snow petulantly.

'Come on, you have your delicious chocolate fudge cake to enjoy. And remember, you will be meeting the other cats.' Mum smiled and squeezed my hand.

'Yes, thank you for the cake.'

The dazzling morning sunlight shone brightly in The Forest. Snow crystals flickered and twinkled in the intense, natural light. This was truly a magical place.

'Sunglasses, Lexi,' Mum commanded, while hers sat on top of her head.

The moment we arrived at the cabin Mum asked, 'Is my nose shiny darling?'

'Nooo,' I replied impatiently, my eyes rolling back in my head. Mum peered into the car vanity mirror, grabbed her powder puff, and dabbed powder all over her face.

Fiddlepuff!

We stepped out of the car and caught the smell of burning wood. A trail of smoke was spreading across the garden from the wonky chimney, on top of the cabin.

Gustav walked purposefully towards us. His heavy black boots crunched loudly on the pristine, crisp snow. He was wearing a bright blue woolly hat, scarf, and gloves.

I froze, transfixed by him. I stared.

'Morning Gustav, it's a little chilly this morning. Are you burning damp firewood?'

Mum's words came out like steamy vapour. The air was icy-cold.

'*Guten Morgen,*' he spoke in a quiet, gentle manner.

'I am off to collect more vood for ze stove.'

'Can I come too?' I asked bravely.

'Now Gustav, please look after her,' said Mum cautiously. She was used to taking care of me herself and looked concerned. She took the precious cake box from me.

'I'm going inside, for a cup of tea with Ellette.'

'Save my cake, Mum.' I paused.

'Pleeeaaasse.'

Gustav fetched a barrow from the side of the old cabin. He emptied pieces of wood from the wheelbarrow and piled them close to the back door. CLUNK, THUMP, THUD!

Gustav took us down a narrow, snowy lane. I walked quickly, keen to see what was ahead. Along the lane, we came upon a traditional cottage. I stood on tip-toes and peeped through the windows. It was dark inside, but something, or someone, waved at me. I was sure of it.

I wanted to ask Gustav if I could go inside. I *almost* had the courage. I felt plucky today, or had the magic begun to work without me knowing?

Fiddlemagic!

We continued along the snowy path, going towards The Forest. Neither of us spoke. Unexpectedly, the light around us began to glow a soft, delicate pink. I distinctly heard giggles around me.

'Who is that?'

Splat! A frozen snowball hit my cheek. Where did that come from?

Gustav removed a glove, waved his hand in the air, and caught a snowball. As he did, the snowball changed colour before my eyes. It was astonishing.

What is happening? Snowballs!

'Gustav, the colours.'

'Anyzing can change if you put your mind to it, Lexi.' As he spoke, the energy around his body shone brightly. It matched the sparkle in his big eyes. *Who are YOU,* I wondered.

'Zey are just cheeky, the forest creatures playing hide and seek.' We walked on a short distance and there before us as if by magic, was a tower of chopped logs. We gathered as many as we could, piled them into the wheelbarrow without a word. I peeped. I noticed Gustav smiling from ear to ear.

'If you are patient, you might see a beautiful deer,' he whispered as he pushed the barrow through thick snow.

He is so cool! I thought to myself.

'Really! I would love to see one.'

I was twirling round, swirling and spinning again and again, in the snow. I felt light. Free!

I swished my red gloves through the luminous snowflakes, then up into the bright blue sky. The cold air clung to the tips of my toes, the tips of my fingers, and my cold pink nose. I was happy.

'Listen...,' he stopped for a moment and stood in silence. Birds filled my ears with their joyful song. I felt uplifted. Something was extremely peculiar in a good peculiar sort of way, but I couldn't quite explain.

We began a slow, steady walk back to the cabin as the snow squeaked beneath our boots. It was turning out to be a most fantastically *unusual* day.

I let out an involuntary giggle of sheer delight, and I could have sworn that someone giggled back? Or was it just my echo?

CHAPTER 4

Goosebumps and Tingles

'SHOO! SHOO! SHOO!'

My heart skipped a beat. I stopped in my tracks.

'Isn't that Ellette's voice?' I asked.

'Ah yes, she always shouts at ze black birds.' Gustav's calm manner reassured me.

'But, zere's one bird I vood like you to meet zat lives wiz Granddad Edric.'

'When can I meet him? Today?' My arms flapped up and down insistently.

He appeared to be deep in thought, stroking his beard. 'No, no, not today, Lexi.'

'Pfft!' The excitement fizzled out of me.

'Let's getz these logs on the fire and have somezing to eat,' Gustav smiled at me warmly.

'What was that?' I blurted.

'Over there.' I grabbed his arm and pointed.

'It's ok. It's a deer, eating from ze leaves.'

'No! It was something black.' I watched intensely, trying to make out the dark shape.

'It might be ze black birds,' he reassured me, smiling.

'Many things will seem strange here because you have never experienced zem in your everyday reality. Zey are perhaps unusual for you.'

'You know zer is real magic here? You can change your thoughts, emotions, your entire reality, in zis forest.'

'Oh! Really. I suppose…' I ignored most of what he said—I didn't understand.

'The cats you will meet very soon, zey are vaiting for you.' His eyes glistened.

'I can't wait. I love cats. I have a cat at home in London. I really miss her.'

'Not long now. Come, let us get back.'

My toes felt numb. Like ice-blocks. It made it hard to walk.

'You are voddling like a penguin.' Gustav chortled.

'Penguins don't walk like that,' I replied indignantly.

Giant snowflakes began falling in a fast flurry, and the light was quickly dimming. We picked up our pace as we huffed and puffed through the ever-thickening snow towards the promise of a homely cabin. On the way, we walked by the mysterious cottage. I slowed my pace to take another peek inside. I looked expectantly for a little face at the window, but no one appeared.

I was relieved to be back indoors, away from falling snow and the icy wind. After removing my wet coat and boots, I threw on my best-loved hand-knitted jumper before going in search of Mum and Ellette. Being inside the cabin felt like a warm, comforting hug.

I entered the kitchen with one thought on my mind—chocolate fudge cake.

'Oh! I stopped at the kitchen door. *Goosebumps! Tingles!* My arms and legs became numb.

I bit my lip in astonishment. Standing directly in front of me were two golden ginger cats with the most entrancing emerald green eyes. They were almost identical and huge.

The cats watched me as I stood in the doorway, gawping. The room held a power, an invisible power, as a light headedness came over me.

Ellette interrupted the unwavering stare between me and the cats—She raised her arm into the air and, with a dramatic fanfare, announced:

'Lexi, I would like to introduce you to Ginger and Teddy. Cats, meet my cousin, Lexi.'

'MEAOW—MEAOW—MEAHA—MEEH!'
Teddy boldly announced himself, then strutted his fluffy, square body towards me. He rubbed against my legs and placed his colossal paw firmly onto my foot with a stomp.

'Oh!' I said, raising my eyebrows. Really? How bold.

'Teddy likes to be the first to say, 'Hello.' He is a real show-off.'

Ellette looked at Teddy, 'aren't you, my Tubby-Ted-Ted?'

'Now, don't tease Lexi. Take your paw off of her foot and mind your manners,' Ellette added firmly.

Teddy reluctantly did as he was told. He removed his paw and turned his back to me while making his way over to the fridge with a determined strut. I was sure he stuck his bottom in the air deliberately.

'Psssss!' Teddy looked back at me with a snarly expression on his furry face. He was not happy.

'I know, you're only playing with her. I know.' Ellette's muffled voice came from behind the fridge door. Teddy sat waiting.

'I don't think we like each other,' I offered hesitantly.

'Lexi, ignore him,' Gustav added.

'Ginger is a gentle giant. They have completely different characters.'

'Have you noticed they have identical white markings on their chests and front paws? The only physical difference is that Ginger is bigger than Teddy,' added Ellette.

'Was their father a Ginger Tom?' Mum asked.

'Yes, Teddy and Ginger are brothers. There has always been rivalry between them, even though Queeny bosses them both around.

Ginger paced up and down, licking paws, cleaning ears, but mostly pawing at the fridge door. Teddy copied Ginger.

Queeny came over to me, rubbed her head against my hand, then stretched up and licked me on the chin. I felt comforted after Teddy's stand-offish greeting.

The tip of Queeny's tail was doing a happy dance. Swaying from side to side.

'Now we are waiting for Tinky to arrive.' Ellette sang with a lilt in her voice.

'Tinky—Puss—Puss—Puss! Where are you?'

A deafening—MEEEOOOWWW—seemed to shake the kitchen walls.

Tinky, the *real* boss and group leader, made her grand entrance through the giant cat-flap.

She trotted regally into the centre of the room, her head held high. She strutted round and round majestically, staring at each of us in turn.

'OK, Tinky-Tinks, you're finally here. Good.'

'Thank you, Madam, for gracing us with your presence.'

Tinky shot a sideward glance at me. Her bright, golden eyes winked.

Did she actually wink at me? Really? They certainly are the most unusual cats. I had a feeling I had known these cats forever…

Tinky was taller than the other cats. Her golden-brown tabby fur was paler than Queeny's, who had the most beautiful marking on her face.

'Lexi, these are my extraordinary cats. We live happily in The Forest together.' Ellette smiled proudly and looked around the room at each one of them.

'Of course, Blinky will appear in her own good time or not.' Ellette's eyebrows raised up in anticipation.

'Blinky! What a cool name!' I blurted spontaneously. A sudden surge of energy took me by surprise.

Ellette and Mum smiled and nodded in agreement to one another. The cats seemed to be nodding, too.

I sat down on a big comfy chair, where Gustav served more of his yucky tea. His freshly-baked muffins, with homemade blueberry jam, were a treat for the adults, and I savoured a massive slice of cake. It was *double-delicious!*

I felt warm and fuzzy with a happy tummy. I knew I was the luckiest girl in the world.

The warmth spreading from the firewood, the crackling sounds of the logs had me nodding into a gentle dreamy state. Oops! I had no idea what time it was. Time didn't seem to matter. Interesting, though—there were no CLOCKS—no TICK— no TOCK—in the cabin. None.

Things were becoming more mysterious by the second and, where was the 5th cat?

Fiddlesticks!

CHAPTER 5

Mysterious Neighbours

WE WERE INTERRUPTED by a loud, *'Knock—Knock—Knockity—Knock,'* on the cabin's front door.

'Who could that be?' Ellette squealed with delight. She had recognised the knock.

She immediately dashed to the door. We heard peals of laughter coming from the entrance hall. A deep, raucous voice BOOMED through the cabin, shaking bottles on the kitchen shelves.

'Hello, my *DEAR Girl*, how are you? Ah! It smells good in here. I'm looking forward to your tasty soup.' The guest spoke in a very deep voice.

Ellette ushered her special guests to the sitting room, giggling with joy.

'Master Horatio. How wonderful to see you, too.'

'Hoot—Hoo—Hoo—Hoooot.'

'What was *that?'* The unexpected sounds surprised Kitty, causing her to tip her glass of lemon and ginger drink onto the oak floor.

Gustav kindly wiped the spill and poured Kitty another drink in the blink of an eye.

'Welcome, come in and meet everyone.'

'Look who's here,' she spoke in her Elvish[9] sing-song voice, 'let me introduce you, to Kitty and her daughter, Lexi.'

'Kitty, this is Granddad Edric, and his wise friend, Master Horatio.'

Ellette gracefully held out her arm and presented her guests with a broad sweeping gesture.

A striking man with a cheerful face peered down at me. His round spectacles propped on the end of his cold red nose. He also had delightfully rosy cheeks.

'Now, who is this, may I ask?' His words roared out from under his long white beard, which flicked up and down when he spoke.

He looked directly at me and said: 'You must be Lexi.'

I clung to the crystal in my pocket. The constant pulse gave me courage. I held it tightly before I spoke:

'Errr, hello, please to…to…meet you.

M-m-mum and I are h-here visiting Ellette. I am her cousin, Lexi,' I offered shakily.

Gustav nodded and smiled across the room reassuringly.

'He vont bite, Lexi,' he added, as he went to prepare the table for dinner.

Granddad Edric looked like Father Christmas. I could definitely smell Christmas pudding.

'Ah, well. Young lady, you will indeed have a wonderful time in The Forest during your stay,' he leant over and patted my head gently.

'We'll make sure of that,' he said, turning his head towards Master Horatio, who was sitting on his shoulder.

'Won't we, Horatio?' The mysterious wise owl also received a pat—pat on his chestnut-brown, feathered head.

Master Horatio had bright amber eyes, surrounded by a circle of pure white feathers. His eyes pierced right through me. It was as if he could see and know all about me: NOW, the PAST and my FUTURE.

'*Voo-hoo-hooooot.*' Master Horatio nodded in agreement, slowly and definitely.

'You can stroke him,' said Gustav, who stood watching over me. I reached forward towards Horatio, then pulled my hand back. I reached again and drew back.

I felt a strong surge to touch Master Horatio's feathery wing. He shook his multi-coloured body, fluffed up his feathers, and held out a wide chestnut-brown wing.

'Yes, just there,' Granddad Edric said,

'Master Horatio likes to be stroked gently. Only occasionally. He is rather a private creature, is Master Horatio.'

I felt BEDAZZLED by everything happening around me.

'Lexi, zis is ze bird I was talking about,' Gustav added, 'now, look at his head— go a little closer—look!' He pointed.

'You can do it if you are villing to try.' He held my hand and guided my fingertips.

I felt a wave of electrical energy ripple through my chest. A wave of jubilation spiralled down to the tips of my toes. For a moment, I couldn't move. *What did all this MEAN?*

'See, he has a definite star-shaped pattern in the middle of his forehead,' Gustav informed me. I nodded dreamily. I saw it for myself and marvelled at Master Horatio.

My attention turned to the cats who were watching my first encounter with this extraordinary OWL. I could feel their presence. We were gradually getting to know one another. Queeny was my favourite, followed by Ginger and then Tinky. I was more cautious about Teddy, and I hadn't met *The Mystery Cat*—not yet.

Ginger cuddled next to me. His soft fur brushed up against my arm. He pushed his head into my side. Perhaps he could also sense the crystal energy in my pocket. We are definitely becoming close friends.

'Ellette,' I coyly beckoned my cousin closer.

'Where's the toilet, please?' I spoke ever-so-quietly.

Gustav and Granddad mustn't hear.

'Go out of the front door, turn left and follow the stone path. That path will lead you to the edge of The Forest.'

'Look for a tall green shack. That's our cloakroom or toilet,' she replied in a soft, gentle voice.

'And mind ze snow, it can become very zlippery,' Gustav overheard.

I felt my cheeks burning. I cringed inside but followed Ellette's instructions, walking as fast as my legs would go. I didn't care if it was slippery.

'Wow! Jeepers!' I jumped back. My eyes alert. A colour appeared under my foot.

I was standing on a large, flat stone that had mysteriously turned blue. I stopped. I cautiously stepped onto the next stone, and it turned green. The stones flickered… I stood very still, unsure what to do next.

I slowly stepped forward again, and pink sparkled under my feet. Lilac was next, while the frost all around me glistened and gleamed.

The lustrous coloured lights beneath my feet continued shimmering. With each step I took, another beautiful colour appeared.

Fiddlemagic!

The coloured stepping-stones LIT the path, leading me further away from the cabin. I ventured deeper into The Forest. My winter boots held their grip.

Each inward breath of icy air hit the back of my throat and instantly chilled my lungs. I could hear my own heavy breathing. I felt giddy.

'*Hurry, hurry!*' I spoke out loud. Immediately, the energy changed. I sensed a pair of curious eyes watching me, yet I wasn't frightened. Instead, I felt curious. I stood still, my body rigid. I let out a sudden yelp of surprise, then a giggle. With a massive sigh of relief, I saw the green shed ahead.

Fiddlewiddle!

Once inside the shed, I looked all around the tiny cubicle. My eyes shot upwards. A sizeable spider hanging from an intricate spiral-shaped web was dangling over my head.

The door creaked loudly, swinging open, determined not to stay closed. I couldn't wait—I closed my eyes—sat down and let go...

I peered through with one eye to see what Miss Spider was doing. When I finally stood up, I was startled by a loud noise outside.

CRUNCH—CRACK—CRUNCH—CRACK.

My heart was racing: '*THUD—THUD—BOOM—BOOM!*'

Now, I was scared. I felt very alone, here in the woods. Who was outside? I tried to catch a glimpse through a small crack in green door. My eyes darted side-to-side, and then—I could hardly believe what I was seeing. Standing in front of the door was a deer.

Her gentle, soft hazel eyes, with the longest lashes, were fixed on the door and me, peeping out at her.

She stood strong and powerful. A light flurry of soft multi-coloured snowflakes fell all around her like she was inside a magical snow globe.

Silence fell, but for the two of us, gazing at one another. Breathing...

'Hello, you must be Lexi, sorry to have frightened you,' she said in a gentle, calming tone. Her breath blew out white sparkling light.

In that instant, I knew I was safe and protected from harm.

'I wanted to introduce myself to you. I am known as The Keeper of The Forest.

My name is Kiara,' said the beautiful doe.

I could hardly believe my ears. This was unbelievable!

'Oh! Umm... Hello,' I said, acting unsurprised at a speaking animal, 'you are a *magnificent*... err, I'm here visiting my cousin, Ellette.'

I let out a long, wobbly, steamy, sigh...

'Ph-uuuw.'

'Ahhh, you must be here to join the *secret journey*.'

'What Secret Journey? Are you a MAGIC deer?'

'I am indeed!'

'I came to tell you, there will be more extraordinary experiences for us to share. All will be revealed, my dear child. One step at a time.'

'My role here, in The Forest, is to nurture and care for all animals and children who visit The Forest.'

'Lexi, children like you, with unexpressed shyness, will never face such challenges again,' she said kindly.

The soulful doe turned away, vanishing in a puff of mist.

I couldn't wait to get back to the cabin, to tell *everyone* what had happened. I skipped through the snow with newly discovered energy and enthusiasm.

'COOL!'

Dashing along, I wobbled and slipped on an icy patch of snow. I stopped for a few moments, took a few deep breaths and, put my shoulders back, and bravely walked on.

A burst of faint giggles from behind the trees urged me to hurry-up. I arrived back safely, with no more mishaps.

My head was buzzing. I was shaking with cold and elation. I felt a fizzy energy inside my body. I had never felt so alive!

CHAPTER 6

The Unseen

I STORMED INTO THE CABIN. 'Ellette, Ellette! Guess what happened?'

The cats immediately sat up, ears pricked, to hear the news.

'Are you alright, Lexi? You were gone for a very long time?' said Mum, fussing.

'Aah, you met Kiara,' Ellette smiled. My heart and head were thumping and spinning all at once. I couldn't get my words out fast enough. Of course, Ellette knew.

'You will never believe what I've just seen.'

'What darling?' asked Mum.

'A deer and *she spoke to me!* It's like real magic. Her name is Kiara. She told me I am here to go on…on a Secret Journey.'

My words came out too fast, yet the adults understood.

'I am so excited about everything.' I skipped about the room, unable to calm down.

'Zat's perfect!' Gustav grinned.

'You'll find out more about Kiara when you meet her again.'

'When will that be?' I asked.

Ellette looked deep into my eyes as she spoke, 'soon, Lexi, soon…'

'Lexi, please remember, it must remain a secret,' Ellette was serious.

I held her gaze. I felt an unspoken 'knowingness' pass between us. Her translucent blue eyes reminded me of the light blue waters of the ocean.

My mind was running ahead. I couldn't contain my enthusiasm. I was doing pirouettes around the room. The adults smiled and laughed.

I wondered—maybe—just maybe—Kiara has the power to make my wishes come true.

What an adventure! I felt blessed to have cousin Ellette, the fairy realm, and Kiara, too.

'Food is now ready, everyvun.'

'Good man, I'm starving,' Granddad patted Gustav firmly on the back, almost choking him on a wooden spoon he was using to taste the soup.

Granddad Edric was first to sit at the table. He stuck the napkin firmly under his chin and waited, spoon in hand.

Gustav placed a large pot of thick vegetable soup in the middle of the table. Completing the hearty meal was a big, round red-skinned Gouda cheese, two home-baked loaves of fresh bread, and local butter.

Granddad Edric cut a large wedge of cheese, then gobbled up his bowl of soup. He was the first to finish.

Not one word was uttered while we ate. It was a very special gathering of new (unusual) friends. I was in heaven, although a bit squirmy and fidgety.

I ate the delicious soup that Gustav had lovingly made. But the cheese… hmm… I was not sure about this cheese.

'Another bowl?' Gustav offered.

'YES, please! The soup is superb,' said Granddad Edric. He held his plate in the air like a flying saucer.

Nobody at the table was finished yet. Mum looked up with a stony expression on her face. She was NOT amused.

She gracefully wiped the corners of her mouth on the linen napkin, folded it into a prefect rectangle, and placed it back on the side-plate.

'Thank you, Gustav, that was good soup. Delicious.'

Granddad eventually finished *all* the soup in the pot.

After eating, we drifted back to the comfort of the main sitting room.

'Where's TubTub today?' enquired Ellette as she carefully stroked Master Horatio's fine feathers.

'TubTub,' snorted Mum, 'who is *that* character?' Mum asked. She stood back a little from Master Horatio. She wasn't fond of birds.

'Ah! Tobias, aka Toby, affectionally known as 'TubTub'. Ellette squealed with laughter.

'Well, he has been a rascal recently,' Granddad said, with a very stern face. He huffed and puffed on his way across the room and flopped down heavily into a chair. It bowed beneath his considerable weight.

CREAK—PUFF—GROAN—OOMPH—the chair and Granddad groaned simultaneously.

'I believe his breed is called an 'Angeln' Saddleback[10] Pig', explained Ellette, 'they are a rare breed, you know.'

'*He's a PIG!*' Mum exclaimed.

'Yes, a naughty one, at that.' Granddad Edric ignored Mum's look of horror.

'He gets his snout into all sorts of trouble.' Granddad shook his head. TubTub sometimes puzzled him.

'He caused havoc at Whistle Cabin this morning,' his cough bellowed as loud as a roaring stag. It startled us.

I sat watching Edric's tummy. It was shaped like a giant beach ball. The cats and I watched it shake and wobble beneath his red waistcoat. We heard a *PING* sound. With that, a silver button went flying across the room, in the direction of the cats.

The cats had been quiet since my return from the green shed but watched me intensely, despite the distraction of the flying silver button.

'Oh dear…,' Granddad looked down at his now gaping waistcoat and scratched his head.

'Well then. Back to TubTub. Now, where was I?'

'In fact, Lexi, he's been very naughty today,' grunted Granddad, 'I told him he had to stay home.'

We waited, poised to hear what was coming next.

'Did you hear Master Horatio?' I asked Mum. I couldn't believe what I heard. I forgot my shyness as I blurted out loud.

'Hear what?' Mum turned to look at me.

'He hiccupped!'

'Imagine. An owl with hiccups!' I giggled with sheer delight.

'Ah, that tells me something,' Granddad added.

'Lexi, when Master Horatio has the hiccups, he is telling me things. He either does that, or he sends me other signals.'

'He is a very special owl. He's not a regular owl—NO, not at all.'

'He is highly tuned into people, all creatures and energy waves.'

'The faintest whisper, and Master Horatio can hear it. He also knows when TubTub is misbehaving and, if necessary, sends me a signal.'

'He could be flying anywhere in the world,' Granddad's arms flew up in the air, imitating Horatio in flight, 'and his radar[11] picks up signals around him, and far beyond that...'

'When Master Horatio hiccups, I pay attention. I am guessing: TubTub has been meddling with something at home.'

'TubTub even broke his reading glasses yesterday. He rolled over and squashed them.'

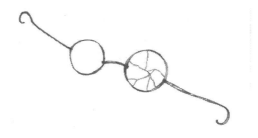

Ellette frowned, 'Oh dear,' the corners of her mouth drooped, 'we'll have to get him a new pair of piggy-glasses.'

'I know he's up to something right now, thanks to Horatio's special abilities. He must have munched all the acorn snacks I left out for him. Mmm...'

"Voo-Hoo-Hoo-Hoo- 'Hiccup'-Hoo-Hoooo.'

'You vant tea?' asked Gustav.

'Yes please,' everyone piped up.

Gustav had added a Bee-Sting cake[12] to the tea tray. My eyes went directly to the cake. I was puzzled by the name. How odd.

Gustav cut generous slices to serve. He told us about the traditional German cake. It had mouthwatering custard in the centre, with honey and almonds sprinkled on top.

I tucked in and soon had honey running down my fingers and custard smeared all over my face. This is definitely my second most favourite cake.

'Yummy—Yum!'

'Pass the teapot—there's a good man,' Edric looked to be thinking while he gulped his second cup of tea with gusto.

'Ah, the wind is up,' said Granddad. 'Master Horatio is leaving us soon.' 'He's flying to the Monte Rosa Mountains[13] in Switzerland. It's time once again. Time that only he fully understands.'

'Time for *what?*' I asked without hesitation. Gustav looked at me with a puzzled expression on his face. 'What IS it Granddad. Can you tell Lexi?'

'Well, alright then.'

'Master Horatio follows the magnetic grid[14] of the Earth, to collect magic dust from the mountains. When he hears me blow my whistle, he returns,' explained Granddad Edric.

Ellette stood quietly, listening. 'I am sure Granddad will tell you more when Master Horatio returns.'

I covered my mouth with the side of my hand and whispered to Mum:

'Everything seems so weird. I feel shaky and nervous. Will I be ok on a Secret Journey, alone?'

Mum put her arm around me and drew me close.

'You'll always be safe.' Ellette came over and hugged me, too.

'*YOU* are part of a new beginning. Please remember: all is well in your world, and always will be.'

'Have faith in the unknown. You are protected and loved.'

I smiled a real smile. No pretend smile this time.

CHAPTER 7
The Cats

Blinky WAS NOWHERE to be seen, yet her whiskers tickled my cheek.

'*Blinky,*' I whispered gently. My cheeks began to tingle. I sensed her energy sweep over my head. I looked up above me.

'*Is it you?*'

A blue-light shimmered on the ceiling.

'That's most strange.' Now I was more curious about the mysterious Blinky.

'PURRNEEOW!'

All four cats sat watching me. They followed my gaze upwards. Their heads bounced and bobbed rhythmically, in perfect timing, up and down, round and round. They watched the blue-light dance along the ceiling. I burst out laughing. It was the funniest sight I had ever seen.

Ginger caught my eye. He walked up to me, looking very cheerful. The purring vibration from his body fluttered right through me, we purred together.

Ginger and I loved cuddles. I put my arm around him gently, then bravely picked him up onto my lap. He sat quietly, without a twitch of a whisker. The warmth and affection between us melted my heart.

'Ginger, you're so cute. I know you would be the best of friends with Prushka.' I gently rubbed his head.

'Are you waiting for a tickle under your chin?' He raised his chin and leaned in. He pressed his strong body against mine. His fur was velvety soft, his face handsome, and his whiskers, long and thick.

Teddy noticed our blossoming friendship. He was having none of that. He jumped up and pushed himself between us. He placed both paws on my knee, then raised his chin up in the air, with a smug look on his face.

'Teddy, it's Ginger's chance. I'm cuddling him first.'

Cat claws were deliberately exposed. Then, a determined swish of the tail from Ginger. He stretched his long lean, tabby arm towards Teddy. It was a subtle warning.

'MEOW—MEOWWWW—,' his strong feline voice, had Teddy off my lap immediately. He wanted no trouble and decided to leave the cabin. Teddy trotted off, towards the cat-flap, in a lofty manner.

Queeny stood up next, and Tinky followed Teddy. Ginger meowed loudly, then jumped off my lap. The four cats went through the cat-flap, one by one.

'*Wanna Play?*' An invisible light tickle on my ear made me turn sharply towards the sound of a high-pitch voice. A sleek black cat dashed by in a blur, and *vanished!*

'Ellette, I am going outside with the cats, ok?'

'Sure. Don't stay out in the cold too long,' Ellette handed me my coat, hat and gloves, 'Actually, I'll come with you.'

'Won't be long,' she called back to the others, whilst putting on her coat, multicoloured hat, and gloves.

'Tinkyyyyyy puss, puss, wait for us?'

We stepped out, and Tinky came running back towards us. The big snowflakes concealed her furry body. She looked like a fluffy, white, powder puff.

'Oh! Tinky, you do look all snowy.'

Ginger and Teddy looked the same. All fluffy and white.

The cats were in the garden chasing snowballs.

I watched with amusement: Queeny carefully placed her delicate paws into the snow. She lifted a paw and shook off the snow before setting it back into the soft, white powder.

'It's at least five inches deep, perhaps more in places.' Ellette bent down to measure with her hand.

'Luckily, it had been cleared, or we would be sinking down into it, and the cats would DISAPPEAR!'

The light around the cabin shimmered. The air around me was pure and clear. The snow glistened like a magical fairyland. I did not want this moment to end.

'Lexi, I came with you to tell you more about my special cats.'

'Oh…' I listened carefully.

'Well, these cats are not like other domestic cats.

'Look at Tinky. She looks like the leader, don't you think? Queeny is the healer of the cats. She will rub your tummy, and PURRR to help if you feel poorly or have uncomfortable feelings. She knows how you feel, she pays careful attention to each of us.

Queeny makes sure we are well cared for.'

'Gosh, that is amazing.'

'Teddy listens to instructions from Tinky. Ginger also listens to Tinky. Ginger is the chatterbox, and the friendliest of the cats.'

After a romp in the snow and throwing a few snowballs, we strolled back inside. The cats followed behind us in a perfect single-file.

Me, the cats, and a shiny new adventure was on its way. I couldn't wait!

CHAPTER 8

Horatio's Journey

THE FOLLOWING DAY, Mum, Ellette, and Gustav went for a walk deep in The Forest. Mum had done very little since we arrived and had 'cabin fever.' It was her chance to explore the area.

I stayed in the cabin with Granddad Edric and the cats. I flopped down on a soft, comfortable chair piled high with feathery, rainbow coloured cushions.

I cupped my hands around a blue sparkly mug of hot chocolate, taking sips of its delicious warmth, as I sat with Edric and all the cats: Queeny, Tinky, Ginger, Teddy and Blinky.

I had no idea the cats listened to every word we said. Blinky watched me from a shaded corner of the room. Her blue-black fur melded into the space, keeping her well-hidden.

'Would you tell me more about Master Horatio, please, Granddad?'

I snuggled under a pink blanket, puffed up the cushions, and waited in the comfortable nest I had created.

Master Horatio was perched on Granddad's shoulder. His head tilted to one side, listening intently. Granddad started telling a story:

'It began many years ago. Master Horatio was a young owl when he lost his way. He hadn't learnt how to properly read the earth's magnetic field.'

Edric stared at the ceiling, deep in thought.

'Hmmm... OR the magnetic field of the earth could have been slightly out of balance on that day.'

'But Horatio landed here, exhausted, weak, and ravenously hungry.'

Master Horatio flashed a grateful, knowing look at Granddad Edric, fluffed up his feathers, gave a loud '*HOOOOT...,*' and settled down.

'TubTub actually spotted Master Horatio first, flying low, overhead. He made a huge fuss about it.'

'When Horatio finally landed, I realised he was in a bad way. First off, he was desperate for water. I put out a bowl of well water and then cooked him broccoli soup.'

'After a good feed, I tucked him into bed made of soft straw and pine needles inside my home, Whistle Cabin.'

'I was aware that young Master Horatio would show up one day. I had been waiting for him.' He gazed at Horatio with genuine fondness. He had become his dearest, wisest, eagle-owl[15] friend.

I stared with astonishment at Master Horatio. He truly was a very rare owl.

'He's an eagle-owl. His family came from other parts of Europe.'

'But—broccoli soup?' I protested.

I've never heard of anyone who likes broccoli soup.'

Granddad smiled to himself. Lexi was voicing her opinion with the same gusto he loved in himself. She will soon be ready.

'He loves broccoli soup, *with* caterpillars too, when they are available.'

'You see, Lexi, Horatio is here for a special task—an extraordinary special one,' he continued proudly.

'He practices deep meditation[16], which develops his inner-vision.'

'You can learn a lot from Master Horatio. Just pay careful attention—but— all in good time.'

I pulled up my nose, in sheer curiosity.

'What kind of things will I learn?'

'Ah, patience, my dear child.' His eyes glistened brightly as he smiled mischievously.

Fiddlehoot!

'Now, where was I? Ok, right.'
he continued.

'Blinky is, I suppose, our very own— mystery cat. She disappears, then reappears. She's no trouble, but you never know where she is, exactly!' Granddad chortled loudly.

'All things in the magic world, beyond this world we live in, can be in more than one place at the same time,' he explained eagerly. 'The secret is you learn to see more than one reality. At first it seems strange and unusual, but eventually it feels completely normal.'

'When you *can't see* Blinky, she could be absolutely anywhere. And what's more, she could be in lots of places, at the same time.'

'Ho-ho-ho.' Edric laughed and laughed...

'Huh! That *is* strange. A disappearing cat!' I was excited by what Granddad Edric said.

As he laughed, Blinky appeared from her sheltered corner, making herself heard.

'Meeow—Meweeoow—Hisssss—

The cats tittered and sniggered, amused at Blinky.

'Hello Blinky.' I said. I think she waved at me with her front paw, then simply vanished, leaving a shimmering haze in the room.

'COOL! B-u-ut *where* is Blinky now?' I asked.

CHAPTER 9

Whistle Cabin

'WELL, THAT'S ENOUGH INFORMATION for now.'

'Horatio must leave for the mountains very soon.' Granddad made a loud grunting noise, then put both hands on his knees and slowly lifted himself from the chair. His round belly was trying its best to pop out though the gap in his shirt.

'Come on, old boy, let's get you off,' he said as they headed towards the front door.

'*Voo-Hoo-Hoo-Hoooo*' Master Horatio knew he was leaving for Switzerland.

'May I go with you please, Granddad? I want to see Horatio fly off.'

'Did you know that eagle owls like to hunt at dawn and dusk. The sun is fading.'

'Come on then, get your coat, but no talking.' He hurried me along, with Master Horatio perched on his shoulder. We walked in the ice-cold air, down the lane, past the purple caravan.

'If you stay quiet, you may see fairies peeping out of the caravan windows,' Granddad said.

I heard a muffled giggle. I watched the curtains jiggle as a tiny delicate face peered out at us and wriggled her nose at me.

'I think I saw a fairy,' I ran up to the window. Was I daydreaming?

'We can come back, Lexi. Come on, hurry!'

'But, but…'

'This is an important experience for you to witness, come on.' He beckoned.

'This is where Master Horatio will launch from.'

Master Horatio sat on the tall bird-table in the middle of the Magic Circle. He ruffled his wings, then stretched them. He shook his tail feathers and fluffed himself out. Horatio knew he had a cold, perilous journey ahead.

I watched Granddad Edric tie an empty pouch to Horatio's claw. Granddad then raised his arm into the air, and, with that, Master Horatio spread his magnificent wings and took flight.

'*Vale Amicus!*' Granddad shouted to Horatio. The owl soared high into the air, above the tall trees, and was gone from view.

'What do those words mean?' I asked.

'Farewell, my friend. It's Latin,' said Granddad.

'Horatio and I are very familiar with Latin.

'Oh. Will he be gone long?'

'It takes about four days if all goes well. He has many miles to travel. Horatio is able to fly at great speed, covering hundreds of miles.' Granddad had a faraway look in his eyes. He seemed to be somewhere else...

Three days passed. We were all waiting for news of Master Horatio's return. TubTub especially missed his best friend.

Granddad invited us to Whistle Cabin, to meet his piggy pal, hoping our company would take TubTub's mind off Horatio.

'Knock—Knock—Knockity—Knock.' Only one person in the world made such a racket.

'I'll go,' said Gustav, getting up quickly.

'Good morning, everyone! Rise and shine! It's a glorious day. Are we all ready?' Granddad hollered.

'Yes, we are,' Mum said as she added final touches to her pink lipstick, which matched her new pink coat with its shiny pink buttons.

She closed her handbag, which was packed full of goodies.

All of us were well wrapped up for the icy weather and ready for an unusual journey into the depths of The Forest. We were heading for the secret location of Granddad Edric's home, Whistle Cabin.

Granddad's bright red jacket, black winter boots and cheerful energy, filled us with warmth and love.

'Kitty first, then Lexi. Come on, shuffle up. Now Ellette, and then you, Gustav, at the rear, if you will.'

Our troupe lined up in a row, one behind the other.

'Follow me, in single file everyone, if you please,' he ordered, stomping through the snow, marching, and humming, at the head of the procession.

CRUNCH—CRUNCH—CRUNCH—CRUNCH

We mimicked a brightly colourful dragon, bobbing along in the snow, with scarves, gloves, and hats in an assortment of colours: Pink, Purple, Red, and Yellow against the white, snow-covered land.

We trampled onwards, our boots scrunching and squelching in the powdery snow. There was absolute quiet all around, except for our boots, pushing into the deep snow.

'Oh, what a glorious morning,' Edric sang at the top of his voice.

'Whoa! You made me jump!' Mum shrieked, putting her hand on her chest, breathing in a mouthful of icy air.

'Even if we are freezing cold, all the way through, I've got a wonderful feeling, it's going to be a jolly, fine day!'

We all joined in with Granddad, except for Gustav. He preferred to listen rather than sing.

'—*Ta-ra-ra-boom-dee-ay—Ta-ra-ra-boom-dee-ay*'

'Oh, what a glorious morning, even if it is bitterly cold, *Tra-la-la-la-la…*'

We sang, whistled, and clapped our frosty fingers, applauding each other along the way.

'That's a very happy song Kitty. Nice to hear you joining in.' Ellette cupped one hand up to her mouth, projecting her voice up to the front of the line.

'Yes! What fun!' Mum glanced back at Ellette before refocusing on the snowy path ahead.

'How much further is it?' I asked anyone who could answer. My legs were getting tired. Walking in thick snow was hard work.

'We're more than halfway.' Ellette's magnetic eyes twinkled like crystal clear pools of blue-green water. She looked like a magical ELVISH Maiden. The sun streamed down onto Ellette's face, which lit-up the snow around us.

We stopped for a moment to take in the beauty of our surroundings. The sky was a perfect blue, with not a cloud in sight. The snow was pure white, crisp, and even.

We carried on, walking in single-file, singing and laughing all the way. Going deeper and deeper into The Forest. Were creatures and magical folk following in our footsteps?

The cats stayed at the cabin. They knew TubTub was incredibly mischievous. Yet, all he wanted in the whole world was to be their friend. Still, they wouldn't have it.

'Mum, is *that it?*' I tugged on her pink coat.

Whistle Cabin was made of dark chocolate wood, and a thick layer of white sugary icing-snow covered the roof. An orange glow flickered from the windows. It was a sight to behold. All my imagination could conjure up, was the smell and taste of Christmas cake.

'Well! Here we are, everyone. Let's go inside, get toasty and sip a hot drink. 'There's plenty of food,' said Granddad, raising his voice as we entered his enchanting home.

We bundled inside to get out of the cold, then shook the snow off our coats, hats and boots. Once they were carefully stored in the coatroom, our bodies began to thaw. We sank into giant, red, comfy chairs that hugged and snuggled us.

The log fire crackled in front of us. We were bathed in glowing heat. Instantly our freezing-cold faces relaxed into softer expressions.

A warmth of colour filled the cabin. Especially RED: red sofa—red cushions—red candles—red table-cloth, on a long wooden, dining table. There was tartan fabric, stripes, and patterns, too, but mostly red. My eyes boggled!

'SQUEEEK! SQUEEEK! OINK! OINK!'
TubTub came tearing into the room. He
crashed into the side of my chair, with a
THUMP and a *BUMP*.

'Oh! TubTub!'

He galloped directly at me.

'That precious pig of mine is so pleased
to meet you, Lexi. He's in very high-spirits
today,' Granddad warned.

'Ellette, would you mind amusing him
while I tend to the fire?'

'Yes, of course.'

'But, remember he broke his glasses a few
days ago? Don't allow him to get too excited,
dear Lexi, or he will be crashing into other
things.'

TubTub ignored Granddad.

'I need to prepare our tea and snacks.'

'I'll give you a hand with that,' offered
Gustav.

Edric and Gustav disappeared to the
kitchen.

TubTub enjoyed dancing, especially 'piggy
dancing.' His trotters skidded, scratching the

wooden floor. He was showing off his moves, especially for Mum and me.

I had no idea how to stop him.

'Duck!' Mum yelled, grabbing my arm and diving for the floor.

Red cushions split open and feathers flew in all directions, passing over our heads. TubTub caught them, flipped the cushions into the air with his snout, scattering them all over the room.

'There are feathers everywhere,' I giggled.

'Ah—ah—ah—chooooo!' I sneezed.

'This is chaos!' cried Mum.

'Enough!' she shouted.

'Atishoooo…' Mum waved a tissue at me, while I sneezed and sneezed.

'Is everything alright in there?' Granddad called.

'Ellette?'

'Yes, all fine—I think,' she smiled.

'Sniff…sniff… Oh! The feathers.'

Fiddlegrump!

'TubTub, stop that *now*.' Granddad's voice boomed through the cabin.

TubTub stopped and did what he was told. Once he knew the game was over, he quietly settled. Well, that was what I thought.

'Lebkuchen (ginger bread) or Berliners (doughnuts), what would you prefer?'

Granddad kept one eye on his pig. But, in a flash TubTub snatched Mum's expensive handbag, filled with tempting treats, and made a dash for the front door.

The front door was ajar, and TubTub escaped, scampering off, through the thick snow. Squeals of sheer delight echoed through The Forest.

'Come on, vee must get ze bag back,' yelled Gustav.

'Oh, dear. My new bag! That naughty pig!' Mum shouted, holding her hands up to her face, in despair.

We dropped everything, grabbed our coats, put on boots as quickly as possible, and gave chase.

'Chaaaarge! Catch that pig!' shouted Granddad.

'What's in the bag, Kitty?' Ellette was panting as she ran to catch up with Gustav.

'Cookies and pine nuts mainly,' she answered, totally flustered about the plight of her designer handbag.

'Goodness Kitty, they are his favourites,' Ellette laughed, then ran on ahead.

Gustav caught a glimpse of TubTub's tail, he was trotting as fast as he could. His short legs barely visible in the deep snow. He gripped Mum's handbag straps in his mouth.

'I vill go zat vay, and block him,' yelled Gustav.

Mum, Ellette, and I went the other way. At last, we managed to circle mischievous TubTub.

'Go that way! No, the other way.' Granddad roared.

'Come on Gustav! Put your back into it, man.' Granddad took a giant leap at TubTub. He flew through the air, took a dive, and landed with a soft *THUMP*, on top of his pal, Tobias.

'Ooof!' Granddad (thinking back to his sporty youth), rugby tackled TubTub and held him in a firm grip. They rolled in the thick snow to regain balance.

We cheered. Tears of laughter ran down our cheeks. The sight of grandiose Granddad and dearest grumpy, TubTub, was a sight!

'Well done, well done!' Ellette clapped her dainty elf-like hands.

TubTub squealed as loudly as his lungs would allow. He was *very, very, cross*. He had lost the bag of treats, which he had claimed, as his. Silly humans.

He sulked all the way back to the cabin. Granddad walked right behind him to ensure he didn't get up to any more mischief.

The icy air was turning my nose, fingers, and toes into icicles. I was happy to be back at the cabin.

Mum was smiling. Her handbag had been recovered, in fine condition. After a wash and wipe, it was as good as new.

In the excitement of the chase, Gustav had tripped into a ditch and twisted his ankle. He was pleased to sit down after all the elation.

'*Tobias*, to your room. You've been very impolite to our special guests.' TubTub was reluctant, but did what he was told. Especially, when Granddad called him Tobias.

'*Oink!*' he replied.

'No back-chat.'

At last. We sat down, took a deep breath, and ate every slice of ginger bread, as well as all the doughnuts.

'TubTub is *not shy* is he?' Mum asked, raising her eyebrows at Ellette. Part of me wished I was a bit more like TubTub. I giggled to myself.

The light was dimming, Gustav had rested his ankle and decided it was time to slowly head back to Ellette's cabin. It had been a very entertaining day!

'Well, we finally met TubTub and what a badly-behaved pig he actually is.' Mum shook her head.

'Bye Granddad Edric, thank you for everything.

Please say goodbye to TubTub for me.' I called from the door.

Granddad waved back, satisfied Lexi's inner-strength was slowly opening up. He was certainly a mysterious Granddad.

'Bye-bye, until next time.' Kitty waved and walked on…

CHAPTER 10

The Golden Pouch

ELLETTE PICKED UP HER flute case and invited me to join her for a walk in The Forest. I was thrilled. Coat, hat, scarf, boots and off we went.

Ellette stopped. 'Can you hear the woodpeckers, Lexi?'

'Listen, can you hear them tapping on the trees—like drummers in a band— wonderful, isn't it?'

She was standing perfectly still, listening intently. She began to play her flute and a beautiful, melodic sound filled the air and my heart. I had never heard flute music before, and I was drawn in as each note touched me deeply.

The clear, haunting sound filled The Forest. It penetrated... The music had a light, high-pitched tone that seemed to be calling to 'the 'hidden ones' in The Forest.

I was floating, flying, soaring, sky high. The sound in the air created a dreamy

stillness. Was I dreaming? I could feel myself lifting out of this world and into another.
I stood swaying, eyes shut, listening, remembering, melting into the moment.

Time passed.

'Ellette, is that Master Horatio, up in the sky?'

She stopped playing, 'Is he back already!'

'Look over there,' I pointed towards the south, 'he's coming closer.'

I ran across the soft, powdery snow, watching Master Horatio circle above. He hovered, scanned the terrain, then began his descent.

What a delight. Master Horatio was back safely, and we would be the first to greet him.

The birds in nearby trees began to sing loudly, along with Ellette on her flute. Everyone was welcoming Horatio home. Birdsong and flute music danced together in complete harmony.

'*VOOO-HOOO-HOOO,*' Master Horatio called to us. He made a perfect landing on a low branch close to us.

We were thrilled to see our wise friend. I noticed the special pouch clasped firmly in his claws. It was bulging. What secrets were hidden in there, I wondered.

We greeted him warmly. I skipped and

pranced around in the snow. Ellette clapped her hands with joy. It was a very happy moment.

'Master Horatio knows exactly what his plan is. He will arrive back at Whistle Cabin at the precise moment.'

Ellette said, tilting her head to one side, listening and waiting.

'If you remain quiet, you will hear Granddad whistle to Horatio.' Ellette pressed her finger to her lips, 'Sshhh—wait.'

She counted: *One, two, three, four, five*—then sure enough, Granddad blew a loud whistle.

'Pheeeeeeeeew...! Phweeeeeeeew! Pheeeeeeew!'

Master Horatio nodded a firm farewell and took off. Horatio flew upwards into the clear blue sky, his powerful wings extended fully. He navigated the tree-tops, then flew higher.

Soon, Horatio was a small speck in the sky. It was the final part of his journey, home to Whistle cabin.

Then the real magic will begin...

We stood in silence, looking up at the cloudless sky for what seemed like ages—I felt warm and fuzzy, despite the freezing cold.

'By the way, I am going into the village to take TubTub's glasses in for repair and a few errands. Would you like to come with me?'Ellette asked.

'Oh! Could we visit Master Horatio?'

'No. Master Horatio needs a long, well-earned rest after he has a good feed.'

'We need to get TubTub his glasses.' replied Ellette.

I nodded in agreement while she placed her flute back in the case.

I was beginning to accept the sound of my own voice when speaking to others. I even *liked my voice* and enjoyed asking questions. It was getting easier. I was pleased.

CHAPTER 11

Finding Queen Jeannie

GRANDDAD WAITED expectantly on the porch of Whistle Cabin for Master Horatio's arrival. He smiled as Master Horatio landed gracefully on his outstretched arm.

'*Saluti Amice, Saluti Amice!*'[17]

Granddad Edric was delighted to have Horatio back. He was also pleased to find the secret pouch, packed full of gold dust, from the Monte Rosa mountains.

He gently removed it from Master Horatio's claws, then safely locked it away in an intricately carved wooden box with a huge bronze key.

TubTub had missed his friend *so much*. His trot quickly turned into a wild scramble. He couldn't get to Horatio quick enough.

'SQUEAK—SQUEAK—OINK—OINK—SQUEAKKKK—he wailed excitedly.

It was a joyful reunion between two good friends.

Master Horatio needed a long sleep. Granddad had his favourite foods ready, which included broccoli soup.

Horatio hooted and tooted to his heart's content, telling TubTub all about his travels. Gradually, one amber eye-lid drooped and closed, followed by a BIG yawn. Then the other amber eye fluttered, blinked, opened, fluttered again, and finally shut. Master Horatio had fallen fast asleep.

TubTub tucked Horatio gently into bed. He covered him with a red fleece blanket to keep him extra warm. He kissed him affectionately on his curved beak and tip-toed away.

Suddenly, TubTub felt very sleepy, too. Both animals drifted off to dreamland. TubTub snuggled up next to Horatio's bedding.

It was easy to tell when he was asleep. He snored 'Like a Trooper'. He snorted and rattled, wheezed, and snuffled, ever so loudly...

Granddad was utterly content. His precious 'family' were settled. He sat down on his much-loved chair and carefully opened the pouch. The magical Monte Rosa Mountain Dust inside the pouch came from a remote area of the mountains. Granddad and Master Horatio knew about the special properties.

The gold-dust had colours running through it. It was incredibly valuable from a magical meaning, which is why it must remain a secret. There were two pure white pebbles, from Monte Rose, in the pouch, too.

Now he must find The Fairy Queen.

Nothing could disturb the atmosphere at Whistle Cabin the following morning. Except for one rather loud pig.

'Nom, Nom, Nom.' TubTub was awake and happily munching on Master Horatio's broccoli stalks.

Horatio meditated in the early hours. He knew how to use his higher mind and had an accurate radar detector to help find Queen Jeannie.

Pointing his thick feathers into the middle of the room and then: *Wham!* A golden surge

of magic-light turned into a hologram[18]—
showing Horatio exactly where to fly to fetch
Queen Jeannie and her beloved cats.

Horatio knew that the Queen was deeply
loved by Granddad. So, he set off early, with
a picture-perfect view of where to find her.

This is going to be one long day, and an
incredible night! TubTub and Master Horatio
would not have missed this for the world,
Granddad Edric , mused. He tapped his
pocket once more to make sure the Monte
Rosa Mountain dust was still there.

CHAPTER 12

The Queen's Arrival

IN THE DISTANCE he heard her:

'La, la, la, la, la, la, la, laaaaa,' sang Queen Jeannie.

'Voo-hoo-hooooo,' Horatio flapped his wings and swooped down to speak with Queen Jeannie. He would escort her back to Granddad Edric , who had the Gold Dust for the Queen.

It was early evening. Ginger and Teddy were sitting at the window. A soft purple mist drifted gently towards them. The mist slowly began to fill the cabin.

Teddy wasn't bothered. He stretched out his back legs, then his front legs, yawned, and settled down on a chair. He wasn't going anywhere.

'Is someone here?' Mum asked, peering over a book she was reading.

Ellette couldn't speak. She stood frozen. She then squealed:

'She's *here everyone*, The Queen is back. Let's go!'

It was clear Ellette was extremely excited.

'*Come on*, it's Queen Jeannie!'

The mood changed from peace and calm to panic and rush. Everyone jumped to their feet, scrambled, and clambered over each other, alert to the highest degree.

Teddy watched from the comfort of his cushion.

'*Gustaaaav*, you're standing on my scarf,' Ellette yelled. Coats were trodden on. Scarves muddled, and wrapped around necks, hats on heads, too big, or too small.

Chaos reigned for a short while. The purple mist kept coming. Purple mist began swirling around our feet and legs.

We untangled ourselves, took a deep breath, and instant calm descended upon us.

We followed Ellette down the path. The cats in tow, except for Teddy. Who would be first to cast their eyes on the enchanting FAIRY Queen?

'Tinkle, tinkle, tinkle.' Musical notes gently touched every cell in our bodies. A radiant vision stood before us. The Queen had arrived safely, thanks to Horatio.

The Queen smiled. Her energy radiated Pure Love. Her vast gossamer wings flicked and wafted around gently. Her deep-set, green eyes held my gaze. In that moment—I was totally transfixed.

The Queen's magnificent gown was hand-made in soft, purple velvet. Her cloak, hand-stitched with pure gold threads, running through the fabric. It was definitely fit for a Queen. She was graciously Royal and elegantly regal.

Queen Jeannie, a pale-skinned,
magnificent, wealthy, ruler of many regions,

including the mighty Rainbow-Star, truly loved making ALL children feel better about themselves. For many, including Lexi, shyness is a daily occurrence.

The Queen loved all Nature, and of course, the cats. She loved the smell of roses and had a beautiful rose garden outside her beloved fairy caravan.

The Fairy Queen was also an expert at sewing and knitting. Her team of fairies with delicate, porcelain faces, too beautiful for words, helped her with her work.

Fireflies and glowworms graced us with their luminous light. A purple veil, like a soft cloud, had enfolded us. The air was ablaze with an atmosphere of enchantment, set off by the glistening snow.

'I have been singing from my heart each day, to bring you joy. No matter what occurs in our Kingdom, I will always see you through. Know that my love for you is very strong indeed.'

The Queen's operatic voice had the majestic trees quivering and vibrating. Snow slid from their branches, hitting the ground with a dull thud. Our bodies shuddered...

Tinky and Queeny were captivated by the Queen's voice and sat quietly, nearby. They adored her.

The words spoken by the Fairy Queen were reassuring, especially to children. She wanted each child to overcome fears and worries forever. She wanted them to understand love, fun, joy, and laughter.

Queen Jeannie held a tiny drawstring pouch made of blue velvet fabric, trimmed with golden thread. Inside the pouch were her magic cards. Each message, written in her own hand. The cards held important messages for the children.

The Queen offered her pouch to the children. They would close their eyes and choose a card from the blue velvet pouch.

'Ask yourself: What do I need to know or understand,' she would say, and the answer would be revealed. The Queen remembered each card chosen by every girl or boy she met.

Granddad stood to attention before the Queen. He was fully focused on her and in awe of her magical, radiant presence.

'Greetings my dear Queen,' he spoke timidly. Granddad Edric proceeded to thank

Master Horatio for making the journey to the Monte Rosa Mountains and then flying through The Forest to locate his dearest love… Queen Jeannie, Queen of the Fairy Kingdom. Edric would do anything for the Queen.

CHAPTER 13

The Fairies

'STOP THAT!' Belle shrieked.

'Ouch!' Trish yelled.

Fairy twins, Belle and Trish, spoke at the same time. Ordella, their tutor, flicked at their wings with her delicate hands.

Queen Jeannie was usually busy with Fairy Kingdom matters. She visited other enchanted forests, attended Palace Council meetings, met with her Kingdom dwellers, had weekly singing practice, and consulted with her dress designer to arrange for new outfits.

During those times, Ordella took charge of the twins.

Ordella had been selected to act as Queen Jeannie's personal helper. She was known throughout the Kingdom as The Queen's Aide.

She ran around for the Queen, flying from place to place, doing chores, shopping, or conducting business.

The twin fairies lived in the purple caravan on Ellette's property. They cherished their home, known as 'PIP,' short for 'Pretty in Purple.' The caravan stood under a magical Rowan tree[19]. Its beautiful red berries drew many songbirds.

Belle had designed the interior of the caravan and took care of that. Trish had a quaintly domestic streak and a healthy way of eating. She loved foraging for edible herbs and mushrooms and cooking the food. They entertained many visitors, who came from far and wide.

There was enough room for five fairies to squeeze onto the long bench. It was covered with exquisite handwoven fabric, with lots and lots of soft, colourful cushions in various shapes and sizes scattered around.

Ordella knew the twins well. She had helped Belle create a wonderful living space, finished off with elegant purple curtains embellished with gold tassels.

The aroma of fresh wild flowers, even in the midst of winter, filled the caravan with a soft, floral aroma. 'PIP' was warm, cosy, and pretty. It was a little piece of heaven.

'PIP' was no ordinary caravan. It was a secret pathway or portal[20] which led the fairies to their own world.

Magic words are repeated, a vortex[21] of energy spins, and the fairies flit through the portal. They arrive at the Fairy Kingdom, standing directly in front of the Queen's majestic, emerald Palace.

Shhhh... it's a secret...

A hefty parcel arrived at the purple caravan. The twins were fiercely curious.

Ordella could order anything she wished for from the Queens fashion designers, who worked tirelessly at the Palace.

Winter, with crisp snowy views, reminded Ordella of Wonderland. It was her happiest time of year. White, Orange, Crimson, Red, Copper and Brown, with splashes of gold, formed the basis of her winter wardrobe. She had gorgeous, shimmering gowns and outfits, specially made.

Queen Jeannie herself had a fondness of pretty shoes. She had boxes and boxes, of handmade fairy-sized shoes, in every colour and style. She loved and enjoyed wearing them all. The Queen was aware that she needed to set a perfect example, for her Kingdom's fairy dwellers. She parted with some of her shoes on Festival Days, adding a golden ring-light around each pair with her crystal wand.

Like the Queen, Ordella ate and drank from personalised cups and plates, which nobody dare touch. Once, a dear friend drank from Ordella's cup and immediately she turned into a butterfly, with the same design as the artwork on her special cups.

'Today is going to be a *great day.*' Belle was in high spirits, which rubbed off on her twin. *'Plop! Plop! Splat!'*

Crystal droplets, heavily laden with snow, fell onto their wings from the tree branches above.

Laughing, fluttering, and spinning their wings dry, the twins stopped mid-air to listen to Ordella before entering their warm, dry home.

'Neither of you will see what is in this box if you don't behave.'

'Ordella, please open it! We promise to behave.'

The twins flew up and over Ordella's head, hovering in front of her nose.

'*Pleeeeaasseee,*' they sang, holding hands.

'Stop pushing, Belle,' insisted Trish.

'You're shoving me,' replied Belle.

'Belle!'

'Trish!'

'Behave. You are making too much noise,' scolded Ordella.

The twins knew when Ordella was angry, she crossed her arms on her chest, and her wings buzzed at bumblebee speed.

'*Bzzzzzz, Bzzzzzz.*'

Ordella waved her crystal wand in a circular motion, three times, which turned the package into a lump of solid wood.

'Now, no one can open it!' Ordella was in charge and *making it known.*

'OK, do you promise?'

The twins nodded in unison. Even their wings were obediently still as they attempted to be on their best behavior.

'We really do promise,' Belle offered up instantly.

Ordella tapped the lump of solid wood, allowing it to revert to the box the twins were so interested in. She carefully opened the precious box. There was a surprise gasp, then deep in-takes of breaths as chiffon, velvet, silk, and lace floated out of the box, spilling over in all directions.

Magnificent handmade garments lay beneath the abundance of exotic fabrics, carefully wrapped in many layers of soft, tissue paper, strewn on the floor of the caravan.

Gasps of sheer delight could be heard. The fairies entertained themselves for the entire afternoon, going through each and every item in the box.

'You each have a new woollen coat, a woollen hat, and matching gloves,' Ordella handed Belle and Trish their new winter items.

'I want the lilac and turquoise ones,' Belle requested.

'I'm having the pastel green and pink ones.' Trish huffed.

'Do we just throw our old ones away, 'Dells'?' asked Belle.

'No, certainly not. Hand them back to me. I will pass them on to fairies from other enchanted forests, who are not as fortunate.'

The twins were *so mischievous*. They flew off into The Forest carrying armfuls of the new outfits to try on.

Ordella did try keeping the twins in order yet never quite managed it.

Ordella enjoyed her surroundings. She took her responsibilities seriously and thrived on her role as the Queens Aide. She loved her daily tasks.

She often worked out new spells[22], using her fairy magic. The purpose of each spell, and it's benefit to other fairies, elves, humans, or animals, was decided upon, by Ordella, on behalf of the Queen.

Ordella inherited her wisdom from her grandmother. Her striking green eyes from her father, and exquisite features, from her mother. She had a shimmer of midnight-blue to her skin.

The spells and potions also protected her by surrounding her body with a purple light invisible to the normal human eye.

The purple shield protected Ordella and others from any dark energy that wished harm or to make mischief with the fairies.

Belle and Trish are not identical twins. Belle was birthed from a blue light orb, on the 27th day, in the month of June, one minute *before* midnight. Trish birthed from a light red orb, on the 28th day, in the month of June, one minute *after* midnight.

The twins carried an extra gene, from a long line of fairy ancestors. This meant they could change their behaviour, and attitude in the twinkle of an eye...

They both had the fairy tint of blue in their fair skin.

All fairies who lived in The Forest developed a blue sheen to their skin.

When they were younger, Queen Jeannie placed a quirky spell on Trish and Belle. This meant that their ears shone a startling bright red when caught telling a fib-fib. If they told a fib-fib, their ears remained red all day. The Queen would not tolerate such behaviour. It was her reminder to them to be honest and true.

'Truth is Light.' She would remind them.

CHAPTER 14

All That Glitters

MUM DECIDED to join Ellette and Lexi on a trip to the local village. Gustav stayed home to check the water pipes, which had frozen, again.

They arrived at the village to discover a Street Festival was in progress. Lexi and her Mum stood and watched while Ellette ran a few errands.

Local folk danced and sang as they moved down the street, dressed in traditional costume, throwing candy to the children.

Ellette returned, grasped Lexi's hand, and began to dance.

'You dance very well, Ellette,' said Kitty, clapping to the music.

'This is so much fun! Wee...'

Ellette and Lexi twisted and turned to the music. Kitty clapped and laughed.

'They celebrate every year in February—an ancient tradition of driving the evil spirits out, after Winter. All the children love the dressing up in costumes and have a wonderful time.'

Ellette had to raise her voice above the music. She stood out in the crowd, with her flowing blue dress and peacock-blue scarf wrapped around her head and neck for warmth. Her leather gloves matched perfectly.

The last stop was the tiny green and white candy shop. I was eager to go in.

The door was locked. The window had no display or decoration, except for an impressive statue of a wooden owl. Ellette rang the bell. We waited until a young woman appeared.

'*Guten Tag,*' Ellette spoke to the young woman as we entered through the emerald green door.

'*Wie geht es den Katzen?*' Grace asked how the cats were.

'They're doing well,' Ellette replied.

This was no *ordinary shop*. This was an enchantment shop, not exclusively for candy and sweet treats.

'Sssshhhhh—watch...' Ellette giggled and gently put her arm around me.

There was a big secret in the candy shop, which Ellette knew about. We had to be in the shop at five o'clock exactly.

An ancient gold clock on the wall chimed five times. A smell of toffee, with a sweet, floral aroma, hovered the air, tickling my nose.

A magnificent gold and silver crystal chandelier, with hundreds of tinkling crystal pendants, hung from the ceiling. The pendants twinkled and shone like decorations on a Christmas Tree. Two yellow wooden toadstools stood in one corner.

My eyes caught sight of a grand portrait. It was of a black cat, beautifully framed, in an ornate gold frame.

'This is amazing,' I commented.

The young woman was at the counter, holding TubTub's glasses. Suddenly, a tiny pair of purple shoes magically appeared onto the glass countertop. A surprise gift for Queen Jeannie.

The assistant wrapped the dainty purple shoes in layers and layers of lilac tissue paper, then placed them into a gold shopping bag. She carefully closed TubTub's new glasses case and handed them to Ellette.

An unexpected loud 'ME—EE—OO—WW—' was broadcast through the shop. *It came out of nowhere.*

'Lexi, meet Blinky, our mystery cat!' Ellette announced.

But—where WAS Blinky?

'Now, let me introduce you to Grace, Gustav's sister, who is the shopkeeper. She is the only one, other than myself, who is allowed to feed Blinky.'

'Yes, Blinky only materialises when she wants her food.'

The portrait of the black cat was a painting of Blinky. It was suddenly empty.

'But—but—how can the frame be empty?' In a flash, there she was. Standing on the floor, in front of us. I was wide-eyed with surprise. Smirks and giggles flooded the room.

'She moves through time and space with ease. She actually teleports[23] back and forth, through different dimensions and realities.'

I didn't understand. Nor did I see Grace put food out for Blinky. It just appeared in the bowl. I looked around for a cat-flap but found nothing.

'*Nien, nien,* she doesn't use a cat-flap,' Grace smiled widely. She seemed to be reading my thoughts.

'That's wild!' I bellowed. Now bellowing was not something I was used to doing!

'Can I stroke her, please?' I asked.

'Yes, you may, but wait until she has finished eating,' said Grace reassuringly.

I took one step, then another, moving cautiously towards Blinky. My heart was racing, my breathing quickened. I wanted to feel her, to *make sure she was real*. She looked up at me, and meowed.

Blinky had strange, beautiful blue-green eyes. Her glossy black coat parted gently between my fingers. She, too, had a white-star on her forehead, the same as Master Horatio.

I turned towards Ellette and Mum, who were talking about going back home, and in that nano-second, Blinky disappeared.

'Wow? Blinky's gone!' I was stunned and disappointed. I looked around carefully. It was incredible.

'Where did she go?'

I turned around and around, in a full circle, searching the candy shop.

'She'll be back tomorrow at five o' clock,' smiled Grace.

'See you tomorrow—Hee hee.'

'Who said that?' I looked around in disbelief. Blinky was back in her portrait.

'No point taking any photos, they will disappear as you take them,' laughed Ellette.

'Really? How bizarre,' said Mum.

'I love this shop!' I said and did a pirouette in front of Blinky's picture.

'Come on, darling. Until tomorrow.'

The three of us, laden with all kinds of treats: sweeties, chocolates, presents, and more, left the candy shop with Blinky back in her gold frame.

On the way back to The Forest, there was little conversation. I was beginning to relax and understand the fairy ways. I also realised, something in me was changing.

We were exhausted from the excitement, but what an *out-of-this-world* experience.

CHAPTER 15

The Queen Speaks

ELLETTE knew that Lexi would soon return to England with her mother. The fairies and 'helpers' needed to act quickly to free Lexi from her shyness and fully introduce her to their ways.

They unanimously agreed that it was meant to be done. Ellette must fetch Lexi at once. She knew that Kiara and the Queen would be waiting for Lexi.

Trish and Belle accompanied Ellette. Lights from the tips of their crystal wands shone along the path. It was a dark night. Ordella began the preparations for what was about to take place.

On Ellette's return with Lexi and the twins, a melody flooded The Forest. It was Queen Jeannie warming her voice. The rest of the group sat huddled together, around a circular fire-pit. Everyone was wrapped snugly, in heavy wool blankets.

Behind the scenes, Ordella attended to last-minute details.

'The pair of you, please help me with the lights.'

'Yes of course, Ordella,' the twins winked.

Many fairy beings travelled from afar to be at this special ceremony. They gathered close to the fire, but only became visible once Queen Jeannie arrived.

These fairies encouraged acts of love and kindness towards all humans and animals. They especially LOVE us when we are *kind to each other*.

They come out to play, using magic when we are sad or confused. They are the *real fairies*.

To Ellette's delight, at the fire, stood Kiara, slightly behind the other guests. She went to her immediately.

'Kiara, how wonderful to see you,' Ellette whispered.

'Hello, my dearest. The secret magic journey begins for Lexi.' She nuzzled Ellette affectionately, then she glanced towards me with fondness.

I stepped towards her and stood in awe. She truly was a magnificent doe.

'You must forgive me for frightening you when we first met. I didn't mean to startle you in The Forest.'

I looked into Kiara's captivating large doe-eyes. Bright and glowing, filled with love. I was excited to be near her.

'Th-that's OK,' I gulped. Kiara gently nudged my hand. I stroked her head, touching her velvet antlers and kissing her perfect nose. This was a precious moment. I would remember it *forever*.

'Kiara you are so beautiful.' I threw my arms around her neck. A smell of earthy fur tickled my senses.

'Come, let's join the others,' she smiled, walking side-by-side with me and Ellette.

'Let us begin,' announced Queen Jeannie, looking at each one of us. Ellette, Gustav, Granddad Edric , Master Horatio, TubTub, Tinky, Queeny, Ginger and Mum, sat before the Queen. I sat close to Kiara, with Blinky.

Grace from the candy shop *almost* completed our group. The other guests sat further back.

'Where is Teddy?' asked Granddad.
No one answered. Everyone knew Teddy disapproved of the 'unknown', of magic, and invisible 'happenings'.

Ellette picked up her flute and began to play. The musical notes created the perfect mood. It was enchanting.

The Queen began:

'Edric , do you have the Monte Rosa gold dust? Please, may I have it?'

'Yes, certainly.' His gentle tone made her smile. The Magic box flew through the air in slow motion. It floated across the top of the fire to where the Queen stood. The box landed softly into her dainty hands.

The Queen emptied the contents of the pouch into an engraved golden goblet. We watched intensely. I waited, holding my breath. What was about to happen?

The fairies also stopped fluttering their wings. A gentle buzzing sound came from their gossamer wings.

'What I offer today is because of Love. Love is the most important gift in your precious lives, whether you be bold, or shy.'
'Join the Life Dance so splendid, you are all that the Universe intended, let your wounds now be mended, your judgement of self now be ended.'
'Let your love not be spurned, there is more to be learned, trust your voice to be heard, it is now time to emerge.'

The Queen's transparent wings sparkled and twinkled in the cold night air. The light from the snow reflected on them.

The magic hour was finally upon us. It was It was half past three in the morning.

'Don't move, don't speak, be still,' whispered Granddad.

The Queen's high-vibrational voice chanted *magic* words. The graceful movements of her hands created patterns in the air. The sounds and symbols turned the gold dust into a powerful, luminescent powder.

The Queen continued. Chanting and speaking in fairy language. The Sylvan[24] language was song-like and unique, her words clearly spoken.

We were transfixed. There was no movement from anyone. The gold dust had become super powerful. If anyone coughed, it could destroy the high vibration. The gold dust had to remain at a certain frequency.

Golden-light particles manifested into geometric shapes in mid-air—breaking into small atoms—bouncing up and down—landing into Queen Jeannie's left hand.

She uttered five magic words:

'Odiastin'
'Carnifis'
'Mocahsty'
'Zenostacha'
'Naatist'

The Queen handed the golden goblet to Ellette. Then the Fairy Queen became more scientific: She told us about 'multiple energies' doing something or other. I didn't understand any of it.

'Oh, we love it when this happens,' Trish and Belle air-somersaulted together.

'Her divine melody is manifesting ze dust into luminous, gold particles—this is pure MAGIC!' Gustav was super-excited.

But—Magic for *what*, I wondered. How does it help children to discover their inner gifts?

I looked up at the sky, hoping for answers.

The stars twinkling in the dawn light. The full moon, low in the sky, was shining brightly.

'Meeeoooww,' Tinky and the cats were hungry. They began rubbing around Ellette's legs.

Ellette nudged me.

'Follow me, cousin. You are about to discover the secret of my Magic Cats.'

'Surely it's time to go back to the hotel? The sun will be up soon.' An exhausted Mum stifled a yawn. She hugged her coat around her body tightly and wrapped her scarf around her head, against the cold air.

'B-b-but, I *want* to see what Ellette has to show me,' I pleaded. I was tired too, but not ready to end this magical night.

'There is one thing you must see before you go to bed. It won't take long.' Ellette patted Mum's hand reassuringly.

'Yes, of course, if you must, then so be it. Please be as quick as you can. I am so tired,' Kitty added.

I had a strange feeling that my Mum knew what was yet to come, but it had been a very long day.

'Come on then. Follow me!'

We headed back to the rambling, wooden cabin. The four cats followed in our footsteps. I knew that my 'quantum friend' Blinky was never far away.

Once inside, Ellette hurriedly opened the four tins of cat food she bought from Grace's candy shop. She filled the bowls then placed each bowl on the wooden floor, in a straight line.

Slowly Ellette lifted the lid of the golden goblet, which had been in her coat pocket. She sprinkled handfuls of luminous, gold dust, onto the cat-food.

'When the cat food and gold dust mix, *real* MAGIC occurs,' Ellette said. She smiled lovingly.

The cats' pace turned into a rapid walk into the kitchen and, without any fuss, ate every morsel in the bowls. I was surprised to see that soon after, they fell into a deep, hypnotic sleep.

Mum and I stood back and watched in amazement. Ellette explained that Grace supplied her with the extra-special, luminous, cat food-mix.

'Wow! It was a lot to take in...'

'The cats won't wake for hours. It's time for us to get some sleep.' Ellette hugged me tightly. We said goodbye, and left for the Blue Rooster Hotel.

I was witness to something magical that would reveal itself more fully, in the morning.

CHAPTER 16

The Truth is Revealed

'HURRY MUM, I WANT TO SEE if the cats are awake yet.' Mum was slow and weary. We had little sleep and too much stimulation. We were both trying to take it all in, yet I was buzzing!

By the time we arrived at Ellette's cabin, I couldn't contain my excitement. I shouted before we even reached the front door.

'We're here, Ellette!'

Mum looked at me with a startled expression on her face. She had never heard my raised voice, to this extent. Mum tingled inside.

'Come in, come in, come out of the cold.' Ellette looked bleary-eyed and was wearing a long, velvet dressing gown.

'Make yourselves comfortable, coffee is on the stove. There are spicy buns on the table. Please, help yourselves.'

'I apologise for not being ready. I'm very tired today. Excuse me while I go and get dressed.'

With that, Ellette, turned and disappeared *out* of the cabin.

'*Where has she gone?* Why would she go outside in her gown?'

'I have *no idea*, darling…' Mum replied wearily. She slowly took off her multi-coloured scarf, fiddled with strands of hair, checked her make-up in her hand-mirror, then settled into a chair with a cup of tea.

I sat on an oversized sofa chair, thinking about what had happened last night. It had been a very random and rather thrilling night!

I stared quizzically at the four cats. They looked different this morning. They had a curious twinkle in their eyes.

Within minutes of sitting down, I was transfixed by the cats. I was curious about them. How could they possibly be changed by eating food covered in mountain dust. My steady gaze remained on them.

Gustav strolled sleepily into the room.

'Morning Ladies, can I get you tea?'

'No, thank you, Gustav,' Mum answered. She wasn't at all fond of his 'Witches Brew'. She preferred lemon, ginger and honey.

Without any warning, Tinky and Queeny slinked across the room, heading directly towards the front door. Ginger came straight over to me and thumped his BIG, front paw, on my knee.

'Follow me!'

'Move!'

Ginger was communicating with his eyes. He glared in an insistent way, his eyes smouldering.

My own eyes opened wider. This was a complete surprise. *What was happening?* Curiosity got the better of me. I stood up immediately, slipped into my outdoor gear, and followed the cats.

Gustav and Mum were in the kitchen talking, while the cats and I slipped out of the cabin.

I closed the front door ever-so-gently. Not a sound. I wrapped my scarf around my neck and pulled it over my mouth to keep out the icy air.

I tiptoed in the snow until I was clear of the cabin. I have no idea how I knew, but I understood: we had to keep this quiet. It was some sort of secret mission.

I walked behind Ginger, who was on his tippy-toes too. I giggled at such unusual behaviour.

He looked like a beginner ballerina!

Tinky and Queeny were ahead of us. They hurried along the path that led to the little cottage. It was the place I had passed several times. The day we arrived, and again with Gustav, when we went to collect wood.

I soon realised that one of the cats was missing. Teddy wasn't with us. Where could Teddy be?

'Oh dear! The door of the cottage is locked'.

It was way too cold to hang about outside. *Now what?* Ellette mentioned earlier that there was a mini-cinema in the cottage. I would go back and ask her if I could watch a film.

Before I made my move, a surge of strong energy ran *all the way through my body*. It vibrated through every muscle and bone. I was tingling all over. I beamed…

'I'll be as quick as I can.' The cats raised their furry brows impatiently. They huddled together, close to the cottage door.

I stayed under the radar and out of earshot. Mum and Gustav, were still chatting. Despite my efforts to keep Ellette away, she insisted on walking back to the cottage with me. The cats wanted our meeting to be 'hush-hush,' but what could I do?

We walked swiftly back to the cottage.

'Lexi, I must warn you, something incredible is about to happen at the cottage,' Ellette said, holding my hand.

'Really, like *what*?' I felt scared.

'You'll see soon enough, but rest assured, you will be *safe*. I can't tell you more. I'll come back for you in four hours earth time.' She looked deep into my eyes and in an instant, I knew I would be ok.

'Here's the key, and the remote for the mini-cinema.' Without a sound, wearing her new rainbow coloured wellington boots, she disappeared down the track in the freezing wind and snow.

Once safely inside, I began to relax. The cottage was furnished rather oddly. Beds, couches, tables—jumbled items in disarray.

'Where's Teddy?' I asked loudly. He instantly appeared in the room, neither meowing or purring. He looked bored and slightly annoyed by the delay.

I leapt on to a large circular sofa-bed. It was ever so bouncy. All of a sudden, I felt giggly and silly.

'Weee! Weee!'

I jumped up and down, pretending it was a trampoline, pillows flying everywhere. Oh! What fun it was.

The cats swiftly removed themselves from the puffy, sofa-bed, where they had settled. They patiently waited. Finally, out of breath, I flopped down, onto the sofa-bed, grinning with joy.

'That was so COOL! Come on, you can get back onto the sofa-bed, now. I am done jumping.'

I patting down the covers. We snuggled up under a wide, soft blue blanket.

I gazed around the room and noticed a strange wooden step-ladder leading up to a spacious loft. There were rows and rows of old books, in neat rows, running across the entire upstairs space. Were they ancient history books? Magic books? Spell books? Hmmm… Then I fiddled with the remote control, looking for the 'play' button.

I stopped and listened. What is that strange noise.

'What is that? Did I hear something?' The cats remained silent.

I kept pressing all the buttons on the remote to see what would happen. I looked across at Ginger.

What are the cats doing exactly? I felt nervous. What was going to happen?

CHAPTER 17

Magic Cats at Work

'OK, MY DEAREST CAT FRIENDS. What are we doing here?'

'When is the MAGIC happening? Is this a secret power meeting, then?' I asked emphatically. I wanted answers.

Ginger spoke:

'With the help of the gold dust, we have powers to take children like you, to the Rainbow-Star region, where Queen Jeannie has her Fairy Kingdom. She helps children discover their unique gifts, talents, and wisdom. It's hidden within each one of you.'

'Our gold shiny whiskers are able to 'sense' children's feelings. Like radar—they search for signals.'

'Once we have eaten the golden particles in the food mix, we fall into a deep sleep state. The high-frequency gold dust works its magic while we sleep,' added Tinky.

'What nonsense!' Teddy said, as he turned his back on us.

'Ignore him Lexi', Ginger said, 'he is always like this.'

'We are aware that you need our help. You are very, very shy and lose confidence easily. We know you wish to disappear when grown-ups speak directly to you. You feel unsure of yourself,' Ginger added.

'We want to change that for you, because we CARE ever such a lot.' Queeny swished her tail affectionally.

'And you turn bright pink when adults talk to you,' said Tinky.

Her fluffy ears twitched, her whiskers glistened, and she lit-up the room with golden light.

'Your long whiskers have turned gold!' I said excitedly.

'Wow! How did you *do that* Tinky?'

'Remember when you listened to Queen Jeannie singing in her fairy language, with her sweet voice?' She smiled nonchalantly.

I nodded vigorously, keeping my eyes locked on her gold whiskers.

'You were witness to magic being created before your eyes. With the help of Queen Jeannie and her magic spells, that mountain dust which Master Horatio flew to collect became high-frequency golden particles.'

'Yes! Yes! I know.' I nodded. I had seen it happen with my own eyes.

'We…' Tinky seemed to be in a trance-like state and spoke slowly and precisely.

'*We are THE MAGIC CATS.*' Her tail swished from side to side furiously. It seemed to be out of control.

'*You MUST listen to what I have to say!*' Her feline voice echoed loud and clear in my ears.

'*The instant we eat the golden dust, our whiskers come alive and we are able to communicate with you.*'

'*The gold dust holds power for a very short-time—four hours, to be exact,*' Tinky's tail swished even more.

'*This allows us to talk to children and find the best way to help them.*'

'That's cool! You are super-clever cats!'

'*To discover your TRUE feelings, you have to be brave,*' Queeny added. She grabbed my attention with her paw.

'Is that why you have gold coloured eyes? Because you eat the gold dust?' I asked curiously.

'*Yes indeed!*' The cats answered in unison, standing proudly with long, fluffy tails in the air.

'*Not me…*' Teddy huffed, but the truth is, he eats gold dust too. I smiled, knowingly.

I hugged Ginger so tightly, I almost squeezed the breath out of him.

'You can actually talk to me,' I sang prodding him in the ribs. 'I can't wait to tell my friends in London. I wonder if they will believe me…'

Ginger stood his ground and glared at me. He looked very serious.

'We trust that you will actually tell no one, Lexi. You are indeed, in a magical place. You will never experience this journey again. You will transform. Please assure us now that this will be our secret.'

'Ellette has special secret powers, too. Have you noticed she never gets any older?'

Queeny chortled behind her paw.

'Lexi, we need to tell you something else: It's about our names.'

'We have been given spiritual names, decided by the Fairy Queen and her Palace Council,' Queeny whispered.

'The chosen names hold a different vibration than our pet-names. The names and their sound, hold a higher frequency. They are MAGICAL sounds, which are required to do this work. It's simply a different tone, more intense.' Tinky spoke in a dreamy voice.

'My name is 'Maitra' not Tinky.
Teddy is named 'Rosco'.
Queeny is known as 'Tilka'.
Ginger is called 'Senca'.

'Really? But, how will I remember your new names?'

'Tinky is 'Maitra', Teddy is 'Rosco,' Queeny is 'Tilka,' Ginger is 'Senca.' Is that right?'

'Yes, all correct.'

Sooo... they had different tones to their names and voices. I liked Ginger's best. I mean Senca.

It's ALL nonsense,' answered Rosco, who was now doing the talking.

'What is nonsense?'I asked.

'Emotions, feelings, thoughts, sadness, happiness...'

'Oh, whatever you want to call it. It's very hard to change, or shift, how a child feels,' Rosco said sadly.

'Almost im-m-m-possible. IMPOSSIBLE!' he shook his head, staring at the floor.

'But, what if we *can* change, Rosco?' I offered.

'PURR...PURR...Purrr...' (The cats still purr and meow).

Tilka's body melted into a soft, squishy, marshmallow-like cushion. She pressed her head into my hands, nudging my palms. She had a way of lifting my spirits, making me feel happy inside. From the very first time we met under the table at the cabin, I felt real joy.

I *know* I am safe with the Magic Cats. I trust them ever so much. For a moment, I wondered how Prushka was doing back home. I missed her.

'What happens next, Tilka?' I asked, feeling fuzzy from the purring sounds. I turned and looked at Maitra. I wasn't accustomed to calling them by their magic names. It would take some time. Maitra gently nudged Tilka out of the way and sat right beside me. Her whiskers tickling my face.

'*Lexi,*' her velvet tone of voice sent tingles right through me, '*think of a time when you first felt dreadfully shy.*'

'Can I tell you anything, even if it sounds silly?
'*Yes, anything, everything.*'

I began:

'I'm especially shy at school. The first time I noticed how very shy I was—I was at a dance class.

148

I needed the toilet. I was desperate to go, but I couldn't put my hand up. I was too frightened. My arm wouldn't budge, but, I knew I *had* to ask.'

I paused for breath and began shaking as I remembered that *horrible day*.

'*How old were you?*' Maitra asked gently.

'Umm, I was five.'

'*Keep going Lexi, you're doing well,*' Maitra added reassuringly. '*We know this is difficult for you.*'

'The teacher—Mrs. Baggle. She was old and grumpy. She reminded me of a wicked witch from one of my storybooks.'

I watched the cats'eyes change. Their gold whiskers began vibrating up and down. Shining and sparkling.

Tilka had stopped purring and was listening intently. I carried on:

'I stood in the class, feeling shy and desperate to go to the cloakroom. A very loud noise made me jump.'

BANG! BANG!

'I was scared! The dance teacher hit the floor hard with her wooden walking stick. She glared at me with a mean expression on her face.'

'*Then what happened?*' Senca asked.

'I couldn't help myself—I wet myself.'

I was shivering. Remembering that day

was too much. I felt embarrassed and sad. Tears welled up and began to spill over.

'It—it—was not my fault—I couldn't help it, but then, I saw the puddle on the floor—Oh, dear—How could I face anyone at school, ever again?'

'Then, Mrs. Baggle shouted in a voice so loud, like thunder.'

'STOP!'

'Don't you dare!'

'Stop at once!'

'Mrs. Baggle waved her stick and pointed it at me. All the girls stopped dancing and turned to stare.'

I gulped for air, tears blinding me. I sobbed and sobbed in front of my new cat friends.

Even though I knew the cats cared for me, I was still ashamed about that awful day. I blushed and cried all at way through my story. The cats didn't seem to mind.

'The other children in my class laughed and laughed.'

'I wanted to disappear. Forever…'

'Oh, you poor child, how cruel, how ghastly.'

'She—teacher—shouted at us—over and over. I thought she would never stop. Each time she shouted, the puddle got bigger.'

'KEEP MOVING, CLASS!'

'DID I TELL YOU TO STOP DANCING!'

'I couldn't dance, I was stuck to the floor. I just cried and cried and I was ever so wet...'

'It's OK, carry on,' a soft PAW slipped into my hand for comfort.

'The teacher had big, bulgy eyes. She stared at me, and I didn't know *what to do.'*

'And then—I—and—oh dear.'

Tilka handed me a few soft pink tissues. I blew hard and wiped my eyes.

'If I wasn't so scared and shy, I would have been able to ask. I am sure I would, wouldn't I?'

'Every child deserves to be treated kindly, and we must treat others kindly, too. We love you so much, dearest Lexi, and we always will,' Tilka said.

A low, sinking feeling, hit my belly. Tilka understood. She rubbed my tummy. I sighed a big sigh, but tears kept rolling down my cheeks.

'Can we move on? Rosco wanted to start the journey, his tail swishing back and forth with adrenalin rushing through him. He loved the adventure that lay ahead.

'Wait! Give Lexi a minute or three—she is not ready,' Maitra insisted, putting her paw up to halt everyone.

'Ready? To do what,' I asked, rubbing my nose and drying my eyes.

'Tell me, Rosco.'

'Sit next to me and we will continue.' Tilka's calm tone settled me.

'I think we should wait. Lexi needs time for what comes next.' Tilka argued.

'Dearest, fragile, Lexi,' Tilka hugged me tightly.

'But, we only have three hours left,' Maitra added firmly.

CHAPTER 18

The Fairy Portal

WE RE-GROUPED on the bed. Rosco found a warm place while I cuddled up to Senca and Tilka. Long golden whiskers kept tickling my cheeks.

Soft, contented, purring, and meows, filled the room. Maitra stood guard at the end of the bed as if half expecting something to happen.

'Lexi, we are about to go on a journey, to the true home of Queen Jeannie, in the Rainbow-Star Region. There she creates change, through her magic, for ALL children. She will help you.'

'We all welcome you into our hearts and love you dearly, Lexi, but now we need to prepare ourselves.'

'How?'

'Come, we'll show you,' said the cats.

'Are you ready?' Maitra asked.

We formed a circle holdings hands and paws:

'We stand together to Unite; here we come through the tunnel of Light.

'We stand together to Unite; here we come through the tunnel of Light'

'We stand together to Unite; here we come through the tunnel of Light'

An intense beam of light flashed like a thunderbolt. It filled the room with bright white light. The walls of the cottage glowed and shimmered.

Circles of coloured light began spinning. Faster and faster. It accelerated more and more—I was spinning in a supersonic whirlwind.

A prism of rainbow colours sucked us up and took us through a tunnel of light. The force *was fierce*, driving us into the tunnel with an almighty surge of energy.

'Lexi, keep behind Tilka and Maitra!'

'They'll protect you!' shouted Senca.

I could hardly hear a word. My hair whipped around my face in all directions. We were twirling and swirling. I was giddy. My body twisted as I spun around and around, until I was upside down. Maitra grabbed me and put me back upright.

Millions and millions of books flew towards us as we entered another tunnel.

'What does *this* mean?' I shouted at Maitra.

'This is known as the 'Tunnel of Knowledge.'
You have to let go all you know and have learnt,
before we can proceed.'

'The books drain all your knowledge.'

The books, with blank pages, fluttered in the air current, collecting up my thoughts at speed. A gust of wind and energy grabbed at me.

I couldn't breathe. I gasped for air—my eyes began to water. Tilka held onto me, and my breathing relaxed, but I was shaking.

"But, why…do we have to do this?'

'To get through the 'Edge of Darkness,' you
have to clear any knowledge. The Dark-Ones
will grab you and use your knowledge to their
advantage. You would be lost forever,' she shouted.

'On our return journey, we get it all back.'

'OK!' I tried to smile, but my lips were dry, stuck to my teeth.

'Forget everything you've ever learnt.
Knowledge can keep you stuck.' Tilka shouted.

Senca flew past us.

'We're almost through.'

Everything slowed down very suddenly. The energy less powerful, the wind less fierce. I quickly got used to the airborne motion. The energy and air around us was more manageable.

'You must fly through the golden figure-8-Gateway, before you enter the Queen's Palace. Tilka explained.

'Follow me!'

'Hold my paw, Lexi,' Maitra held me close. In front of me, I felt a powerful surge of energy coming from a bright, golden light in the shape of a perfect 8. The thrill was immense. A feeling I had never experienced before. It was mega-cool!

'Let's go!'

Whoosh—with ease and grace, we flew around the perfect 8, then through the gateway—to the other side. I didn't freeze-up. I made it through!

The darkness struck immediately. It turned pitch black.

'Hold on to Maitra and Tilka,' shouted Senca. I held their paws firmly. Figures flew past us. I shuddered at their menacing faces and dead eyes, that watched us very closely.

'Quick this way, hurry!'

'Faster—Faster!' shouted Senca.

'The shadows are getting too close. I fear they are going to strike,' he warned.

'Oh no! They've grabbed Rosco.' Senca hissed loudly but kept his thoughts to himself. Rosco was removed and disappeared into the Darkness...

STOP!

'We've got to rescue him. Go back, go back!'

Senca's fur stood on end, all the way down to the tip of his tail. He made a quick decision.

'I am going back to help Rosco.'

'Maitra and Tilka, head to the light with Lexi. I'll meet you back there, with Rosco.'

In a flash, Senca had vanished.

On the horizon a beautiful bright white light appeared—Queen Jeannie—Queen of the Fairies, was waiting at the entrance of the spectacular Rainbow-Star Region. Ahead of us stood the majestic Emerald-Crystal Palace, Queen Jeannie's official residence.

There was great relief. We had made it. Our little group beamed with JOY.

What a triumph!

CHAPTER 19

The Fairy Kingdom

'FOLLOW ME.'

The Queen flew on ahead, up towards her grand Palace.

'Are we going up there?' I asked. I didn't mind the long climb up the enormous staircase, towering in front of us, but I was tired, overexcited, and nervous.

I had to manage it, somehow. There was an unexpected flitter in the air above me, like dragonflies flapping their tiny wings. I looked up, and to my surprise, a voice.

'Hello Lexi. I'm Belle this is my twin sister, Trish. Pleased to be acquainted,' they giggled simultaneously.

'I *knew* you were real. I knew it.'

My eyes darted around inquisitively. I battled to keep the twins in my sights, as they flitted and flew hither and thither.

'*Careful, Lexi, watch your step.*' Tilka grabbed my arm.

'I can't believe we are in the Queen's

Kingdom and that the purple caravan fairies are real!'

'*They are,*' answered Maitra amusedly.

As I climbed the steep staircase, I gazed left and right, keeping my eyes on the fairy beings.

All around were shops and dwellings in higgledy-piggledy rows. They were teensy but oh-so grand. There were all sorts of shops with playfully-painted exteriors: tailors, dressmakers, milliners, handmade shoes, and a shop with a giant bow around it that sold ribbon and lace.

I looked around as far as my eyes could see. I was astonished and amazed at the Fairy Kingdom. Utterly beautiful!

The twins flew slightly ahead. I noticed their ultra-fine, silky wings change colour. Blue to red, then purple with yellow, now green, back again to blue. It was astonishing.

'Lexi, did you know that we can change anything, even emotions, or thoughts, in a nano- second? We've been secretly helping you since you arrived in Ellette's world. Have you noticed any changes in yourself?' asked Trish.

'How about confidence?' added Belle.

Two pairs of pretty, slanted eyes peered at me intensely, waiting for my answer.

'Powerful Lexi, that's you. Incredible Lexi. That's you, you, you,' they sang over and over, in perfect harmony.

'Oh, along with Gustavson. Not forgetting him.' Belle blurted.

'Gustavson?'

'Yes, Gustav is a true elf, of the Elven clan, a Wood Elf, actually.'

'Really?'

'Yes.'

'We change thoughts, we change feelings too. You're not dreaming. Magic is beaming at you all the time, whether you are awake or asleep.'

'I did notice something different—was it you?'

'Yes,' the fairies giggled and giggled.

'Today's going to be another one of those special days we have in our Kingdom,' said Belle excitedly.

'Come on, let's catch up with Queen Jeannie.'

Trish beckoned to me as she went flying up the steep staircase. For no reason, Belle flew back and pinched my ear.

'Ouch... why?' I grabbed at it, rubbing furiously.

'Leave Lexi's ear alone. You need to be nicer and kinder, remember…'

'Ordella's not here; you can't boss me about like that.' Belle huffed.

'Pinky friends?' They laughed, then gripped fingers affectionately. Yes, it was going to be a very special day at the Fairy Kingdom.

CHAPTER 20

The Palace

AT THE TOP OF THE STAIRS, we approached a grand entrance. Two exceptionally tall guards appeared. They swung back the heavy, iron-studded, wooden doors, letting us pass through.

Queen Jeannie nodded to the guards as they stood to attention. The Palace Guards were noble-born warriors trained to serve the Queen.

They were dressed in long, embroidered, purple tunics, trimmed with gold cord and shiny buttons. Soft, floaty trousers were worn tucked into ankle-high boots. Each guard carried a long, crystal wand and a finely crafted wooden sword on their person.

'Ma charra faa ARIANA ay ALORA.' The Queen greeted them both.

We followed the Queen along a wide, cobbled path, then through a majestically carved archway. We arrived at another ancient doorway.

We stepped directly into a high-ceilinged, rectangular vestibule, which was ornately decorated. It was a vast space, taller than it was long. I had never been inside a fairy palace before.

The Queen announced: 'This is my true home. It is also for the use of my fairy family and many companions.'

Belle and Trish nodded in agreement. Their wings turned silver-blue to compliment the colour of the Queen's extended wings.

The gracious Queen of the Fairies led us into a Grand Hall. A colonnade of tall, marble pillars ran along each side of the vast hall. Each pillar was carved from a single piece of green forest marble. The magnificent pillars gave a feeling of earthiness and strength.

There was a huge, elaborately carved fireplace, big enough for us to hide in. The fairies could fly in and out of the chimney when the fire was not lit. This was the Queen's favourite room, to relax and entertain.

'Welcome to my residence, named 'The Palace of Truth.' This is where you reveal your true feelings, if you are willing to trust and explore your inner-self.'

The wise Queen bowed her head ever so slightly. She then turned to the cats.

'Where are the others, Maitra?' There was a note of concern in her voice.

'*Rosco was captured by the Dark-Ones.*'

'*They stole his knowledge. He didn't clear his thoughts in time to pass through the Gateway.*'

'*Senca has returned to The Forest to find Master Horatio. He has, as you know, remarkable radar vision.*

We must find where the Dark-Ones have taken Rosco.' Maitra sounded worried.

'We only have two hours left. The magic dust will be weakened after that time,' Tilka reminded the Queen.

I shuddered, thinking about the scary 'Dark-Ones.' What would they *do* to poor Rosco?

The Queen spoke to me in a dignified, kind voice:

'Lexi darling, all five Magic Cats have to be with us to allow the magic to work. We wish to rid you of your shyness forever. I will do all I can for you.' I curtsied respectfully.

'Very well. Senca and Rosco are clever cats, they will know what to do. The Dark-Ones cannot 'see' or are 'aware' of energy or emotions, yet they are intelligent,' she laughed softly.

'Who *are* the 'Dark-Ones' exactly?'

'They hunt us for our vitality and make use of our high Frequency,' she said, shaking her head, 'in other words, they wish to use our energy and power.'

I felt queasy at the thought.

'You can change your thoughts, Lexi.' Trish brushed past me and tapped me on my shoulder with her wand.

'They truly despise any form of music or singing, too dear Lexi. It holds a power over them.'

Can I change a thought? How? I wondered.

In the centre of the Great Hall stood an exceptionally long, amethyst dining table. An ancient tapestry cloth was laid over it.

Ordella had arranged the table settings. A spread of delicious food was thoughtfully laid out for our enjoyment. To start, there were tall, engraved goblets, filled with crushed berries, piled high with vanilla ice-cream. Beside the goblets sat a large, golden bowl filled with wild, sweet strawberries. Plus, a traditional Honey Cake. The Queen's favourite.

'Thank you, Ordella, perfect as always…,' said the Queen.

'I love seeing the table sparkle and shine with deliciousness!'

With that, Ordella flew hastily back to the kitchen.

'Come, feast yourselves. You must be hungry after your long journey,' said Queen Jeannie, walking towards the table.

'Oh! I love fairy-sized finger food. Look,

canapes and stuffed wild mushrooms,' cheered Trish.

'*Ah, you will be well fattened up,*' giggled Maitra, amused at the ice-cream and cakes on the table. She discreetly swept her paw across the thick, whipped cream topping and cleverly licked her paw before anyone noticed.

Everyone tucked in, eating daintily but enjoying every exquisite morsel. The food looked so pretty! It was decorative and rather good to eat, too. We filled our tummies with the delicious finger-food, and yummy chocolate frothy drinks. What was in that drink? A little bit of Magic, perhaps? Hmmm…

Meanwhile, at Whistle Cabin.

'*Master Horatio! Master Horatio, we urgently need you. Please hurry!*' Senca shouted into Horatio's ear.

Horatio was in the middle of meditation. He was completely unshaken by Senca's outburst.

'*Master Horatio, open your eyes, are you in there?*' asked Senca, carefully lifting an eyelid and peering into his large amber eyes, eager to get a reply.

'*Come on, wake up,*' Senca tugged at Master Horatio's wing, which caused him to wobble, almost falling off his special meditation-perch.

Horatio opened one eye, '*WOOOOO—HOO,*' then the other eye, followed by a long—'WHEEW'—out-breath.

'Now, now. What *is* all this fuss about?' Ellette asked, appearing out of *nowhere*.

'Senca, what are you up to? Where are the others?'

'*Ellette, we've got a serious problem. We won't be able to help Lexi. Rosco was captured by the Dark-Ones.*'

'*We know Master Horatio would be able to see where they've taken him.*' Senca was very worried.

'Well, we had better hurry, this is serious!' Ellette stroked Senca's paw to comfort him.

Master Horatio stood tall, ruffled his feathers, sat back down, and went to his inner vision place to find Rosco with a faraway look in his eyes.

'Now… let me have a good look…'

'Master Horatio—please—PLEASE— we must locate Rosco. Time is fleeting!' Ellette asked pleadingly.

'*Vooo-hooo*—Aah, I see Rosco—They have him in the region called, Dark-Star. Everyone who lives there is stuck in negative emotions and thoughts and can't get out.'

Tsk...tsk... he mumbled.

'We need to act fast,' said Horatio.

'How do we go about rescuing him?' Senca asked. He looked at Ellette, then Horatio, for answers.

'Senca, this is urgent. Hurry! We must find a way...' said Ellette.

The animals of The Forest were aware that Ellette and Granddad Edric were the only ones who could hear Master Horatio speak. They all kept quiet and listened...

'Oink, oink, oink...,' TubTub was listening too, he wanted to be part of the Rescue Mission.

'Not *now*, TubTub,' snapped Ellette.

'Before I forget, let's take gold dust with us, just in case. Earth time is catching up on us.'

CHAPTER 21

Rescue Mission

ELLETTE AND SENCA WAVED farewell to Master Horatio, and TubTub.

They ran to the cottage, holding hand and paw tightly. They were prepared to do whatever they could, to rescue Rosco.

'Ready?' Ellette looked at Senca.

'Yes,' he said, 'let's do it.'

'We stand together to Unite, here we come through the tunnel of Light.'

'We stand together to Unite, here we come through the tunnel of Light.'

'We stand together to Unite, here we come through the tunnel of Light.'

With the blink of an eye, they swept through the rainbow tunnel, travelling at lightning speed. They flew swiftly past the 'Books of Knowledge' and out into the GOLDEN sphere. Then, through the 8-Gateway.

Suddenly, complete darkness surrounded them.

'Rosco *must be rescued* from the Dark-Ones.'

'Yes, we will find him.' Senca was ready to fight. They flew on as fast as they could. Ahead, they saw them. The Dark-Ones. An evil looking bunch of beings. A smirk and cackle from a face of disgrace confronted Senca. It looked gangly with long, crooked fingers. This called for immediate action: There was a loud—CRACK—bright white light, pierced through the Dark-Ones, guarding the entrance to DARK-STAR. With another almighty blast of blinding light, the Dark-Ones turned and fled. Ellette had used *her* powers to rescue Rosco.

In the distance, they could see Rosco sitting inside a damp, dark room. It was part of an old ruin. He was their captive.

Senca charged forward towards him, colliding with another one of the guards. He could feel the coldness of its skin even through his thick fur. He managed to spin, swerve, and dive, to cause confusion. Ellette called upon her Higher Powers and blasted the Dark-One, with a beam of powerful, white light.

The Dark-One, disorientated by the intense light, spiraled downwards, letting out a high-pitched, blood-chilling shriek before disappearing into the depths of the unknown. Senca made a gallant dash for Rosco.

'Got you!' Senca's fur was standing on end.

He was the warrior, he would save his brother from the clutches of the sneaky ones.

'I thought you were never going to find me!' Tears ran down Rosco's furry cheeks. They hugged.

'Quick, Ellette is waiting.'

Arm in arm, they joined Ellette at the entrance to Rainbow-Star.

'Won't Ellette be looking for us? How much longer will we be here, Maitra?'

I could not believe I was sitting in the Queen's Palace, eating a bowl of ice-cream.

I had completely lost track of time. Maitra watched with big eyes as I put another spoonful of rainbow ice-cream into my mouth.

'It shouldn't be long now.'

In the next instant, as if out of nowhere, they were back.

'We're here—we're here,' yelled Senca.

'We've freed Rosco!'

'Aah…finally! I had concerns,' The Queen floated to the centre of the group.

'My dearest sweetheart cats, you're here, and Ellette too—hello my darling.'

Queen of the Fairies, and Ellette, kissed each other gently on each cheek.

'Rosco, next time, I will be forced to cast a spell over you. You placed Lexi and the other cats in grave danger!'

Queen Jeannie was not amused. Rosco bowed his head in shame before the Queen. His tail sat perfectly still.

Now that all the cats were present, gold dust was generously sprinkled into bowls. They ate it all up without a word, then settled down on invitingly soft cushions instantly looked dreamy and relaxed.

Queen Jeannie led us from the Great Hall into an exquisite emerald green Ballroom. Old Master paintings of noble fairies and elves hung on the walls.

'Who are they, Ellette?'

'I will tell you later,' she whispered, 'listen to Queen Jeannie.'

'Lexi.' Queen Jeannie stepped forward and looked deep into my eyes.

'Would you come and sit next to me?' she summoned me with a graceful gesture.

I sat upon a gold velvet cushion on a grand throne-like seat. I was a mixture of happy and nervous. Ellette held my hand.

'Lexi, you've reached a place, where as a child, you can begin to understand Real Truth.' A wise look spread across the Queen's face.

'Firstly, I ask you to look closely at this crystal-star.' Queen Jeannie was holding a clear crystal-star in her small hands. She leant towards me.

'Notice there are five-points to this star. Now, we lightly tap on each one, with our finger tips,' she explained.

I stared at the crystal-star. I could feel no special magic, but I *could see* rainbow lights glistening at each point of the star.

I was entranced by the myriad of colours that glimmered around it, like a halo. There were also colours shimmering inside the crystal-star.

'The crystal-star dispels children's fears, while the rainbow-light flows through their bodies,' she said gently.

'In fact, when Ellette was a young girl, she

too, had trouble with shyness, but we settled that concern long ago.'

'Yes, that's true,' answered Ellette, 'as we mature, we learn to understand how we react, in different situations.'

'Crystal-tapping releases your troubled thoughts. In your case: your shyness has stopped you from following your dreams. So—you must release that bothersome difficulty—let it go.'

'How do I manage that, please?' I asked.

'It's the same movement as patting a cat.'

'You simply tap 2-times, at each point.'

'Shall we begin?' I nodded.

The cats had gathered, creating a magic circle around Lexi. Blinky was sitting at the top of one of the tall, marble pillars watching.

'I want you to remember: being shy is neither good nor is it bad, it just IS. What you will do dear child, from now on, is not allow it to bother you. You won't mind being shy anymore.'

The Queen paused. 'Ellette, how much time do we have left?'

'One hour.'

'Let us continue. Think back to the day you felt too shy to put up your hand, to ask teacher if you could go to the cloakroom.

What made you too scared, to ask?'

She knew exactly what Lexi was about to say, due to her inner-powers—her insights went deep. The Queen patiently allowed Lexi time to answer in her own way.

'Mrs. Baggle scared me the most. She yelled at us a lot. That day she yelled louder and louder.'

'I wanted to stop dancing. I needed to go to the toilet.'

I flushed with embarrassment as I answered. It was a very uncomfortable subject, but Queen Jeannie was loving and kind. It was surprisingly easy to tell her my sad tale.

'Now, tell me, what was good about your dance class?'

'I did really well. I learnt all my steps because I loved dancing.' My throat felt parched.

The three of us tapped one of the points of the crystal-star. Immediately, seven rainbow-colours, burst out through the crystal-star and swirled around us.

'Now Lexi, repeat after me—then gently touch each point, twice with each finger,' she said, showing me how to do it properly, while holding her crystal wand:

'Crystal of Light shine so bright, dazzle and frazzle old Mrs. Baggle.'

'Now, listen and repeat after me.'

'Thumb on the Senca-Star point—
tap, tap.'

'First finger on the Rosco-Star point—
tap, tap.'

'Index finger on the Tilka-Star point—
tap, tap.'

'Ring finger on the Maitra-Star point—
tap, tap,'

'Little finger on the Blinky-Star point—
tap, tap.'

Energy fired out in bursts. It circled around us, and swept into the long, grand hall. Bouncing rays of light and colour filled the space. It shone everywhere. It swirled and danced, wrapping a myriad of colours around me.

The fairies, including Ordella, celebrated. Somersaulting and sweeping through the air, in sheer delight. They flitted about in every direction, chasing the coloured beams.

'Each tap on the crystal-star, also lights up the cats whiskers. Watch them turn gold,' whispered Ellette.

I looked on in awe.

'What's the Queen saying, now?'

'It's called Light Language.'

'Oh—Wow—ee!' I shuddered… the energy and colour washed over me, and through me…

'Take a deep breath and relax,' said the Queen in a soft, dreamy voice.

'I want you to think of Mrs. Baggle.'

'Let me know what is happening.'

'Nothing.' I began to giggle.

'Tell me how you feel?' Queen Jeannie urged.

'I feel warm and tingly.' I was still giggling (I couldn't stop).

'Now, hold the crystal-star with both hands. I will do a final energy clearing.'

'Close your eyes and instead of Mrs. Baggle, see ME, Queen Jeannie, in her place.'

She gently waved her crystal wand over my head. It tingled and prickled.

'Nothing, still nothing.' I answered with delight.

'This is where you open up—allow—Now, step forward, open your heart, and speak.'

'Allow…'

'You will soon know that being shy is not

a problem anymore. You will remain happy, knowing that you are as perfect as you are meant to be.'

'And, WE all LOVE you, dear Lexi,' whispered the Queen.

'As soon as you feel good about who you are, shyness will disappear.'

'That sinking feeling has gone. I really don't have any feelings that upset me, or frighten me anymore. I know I can speak up for myself.'

The cats released the circle, hugging me, one at a time. Senca paw-pumped with me, followed by Rosco. That made me giggle even more.

'This is very special occasion for you, Lexi. Only at the Palace of Truth, can such rapid change take place, using the Queen's healing power, and the tapping energy-work[25].' Ellette explained.

'The energy generated from all 7-rainbow colours, via the crystal-star heals you, and opens you up to ALL your heart desires.'

The cats burst into joyful song:
She no longer feels shy,
She doesn't need to cry,
She can let out a sigh,
And say goodbye...

'*Meeoow,*' Tilka added.
'*Meeoow,*' Maitra added.
'*Meeoow,*' Senca added.
'*Meeoow,*' Rosco ended.
'*Rooaruh,*' Blinky added.

'Lexi, you look different,' commented Ellette.

'Do I? I feel slightly light-headed—a little dizzy.'

'Queen Jeannie, you have incredible powers, thank you,' I smiled happily and did a deep curtsy.

'It is you, my dearest darling, that transformed your own inner-self,' she replied. A remarkable emerald light radiated from her eyes.

'Finally, you will speak for yourself.'

'What a wonderful adventure you've had, Lexi. Are you ready to make your way back to The Forest to tell your Mum all about it?' asked Ellette.

I had a very different feeling inside. I had no concern about shyness. I knew that if I ever did feel shy, it would be perfectly fine.

CHAPTER 22
Precious Gifts

'WE NEED TO HURRY! We must get back to The Forest.'

Ellette knew the power of the gold dust was running out, and soon, the cats' whiskers would sparkle no more.

'Dearest cats, please take another mouthful before we leave, it will add extra 'whisker time' to our journey home.'

Maitra arched her back, Tilka yawned, Senca stretched out his back legs, Rosco lengthened his front legs in a good, long stretch, and, Blinky gracefully extended her claws, revealing long sharp nails.

They were aware their work with Lexi was coming to an end.

Rosco groaned. *'Do we have to?'*

Tilka gave Rosco a cold stare. Her look was enough to shut him up.

'Did you hear that noise?' I said.

'It wasn't me,' grinned Senca, yawning lazily.

A feather-like feeling tickled my skin. Something, or Someone, was next to me. I sensed their energy. I tingled all over.

'Is it you Blinky?'

'Oh, I get it now! That face I saw through the window at the cottage when Gustav and I were collecting wood. It was you.' I laughed.

'*Hee—hee—hee.*' Blinky winked. Then— *Whoosh*—Blinky disappeared.

'Blink, and she's gone.' Belle giggled and giggled. What a surprising cat.

The Queen, Ellette, and the fairies joined us at the main entrance to the Fairy Kingdom. The Queen stepped forward and touched my shoulder. I felt I was being lifted above the ground—floating—flying. I had to wriggle my toes to make sure I was still standing on earth.

'I will be escorting you back to the edge of The Forest. Belle and Trish will be travelling with you.'

'Lexi dear, I want you to remember, I will be with you always. The white light from the centre of my crown is the brightest light of all. It can light up *any* darkness,' whispered the Queen.

'Always remember the happier you feel, the more loving you are, there is less chance of any negative energies being attracted to you.'

Ariana and Alora gathered us together at the main entrance, checking that we were ready for the journey.

'Whatever happens, we must not let the 'Dark-Ones' capture Rosco again,' Senca said cautiously. He cared deeply for him.

Twitching her whiskers, Tilka raised her paw to grab our attention: *'As we leave, I suggest that we split into two groups. Maitra, Lexi, Ellette, and I, will distract the dark- ones.'*

'We will fly ahead, going to the right. Our Queen, Rosco and Senca, should fly on the left.'

'Good idea, Tilka,' said Queen Jeannie. The Queen knew that her powers, and the skills of her warriors, Ariana and Alora, could wipe out any dark energies with ease, but she gave Tilka her moment.

'Koora ye mana, sam ey a ma choo.'

The warriors spoke. Then led the way out of the Kingdom, flying straight through the main entrance and on towards the tunnel, the figure of 8, where often, the 'Dark-Ones' hid.

Queen Jeannie had the Rainbow Warriors, Ariana and Alora, close to her. The mighty warriors were well respected. Known as the 'Star-Warriors' throughout the Fairy Kingdom.

'Stay close,' Ariana spoke.

They ushered the eight of us, including Blinky, through the darkest area at speed, without any problem. We gained back our 'knowledge' and flew through the figure 8-Gateway and the tunnel. Shadows hovered all around us.

Queen Jeannie and the Rainbow Warriors bid us a final farewell once we were out of harm's way.

'Thank you! We love you. Bye.' Our muffled yells followed them, they made a sharp turn and flew away at top speed.

Before I knew it, we had landed back safely, inside the cottage. Fur, whiskers, paws, clothes, legs, boots, hats and hair, landed in a discombobulated tangle— bump—bump—bumpity—bump.

'We are home. All are safe.' Ellette smiled.

Belle and Trish decided to go directly to the purple caravan, near to Ellette's cabin.

The colour of the walls in the cottage changed back to a soft grey. At that exact moment, the gold dust ran out. The cats'

magic powers were no-more. They reverted back to their usual behaviour and pet names—Tinky, Queeny, Ginger, and Teddy.

'Meoow—Meoow' Tinky was sad. She could no longer speak.

'I know, Tinky, it's not fair. Come on, let's get back to the cabin and have something to eat,' said Ellette as she took out her key to lock the door of the cottage. It was indeed a place of *real magic*.

CHAPTER 23

The Final Curtain

TAP—TAP—TAP—TAP— A firm tap was coming from one of the windows.

'What was that?' Mum asked.

'I will go and see what zat is, there are alvays animals vandering around from ze forest.'

Gustav put on a coat and dashed outside. I saw Kiara peering through the front window as he opened the door. Her eyes shone brightly. She carried an aura of wonderment about her. It touched all of us, right through the double-glazed, frosty windows.

Gustav walked up to Kiara and greeted her with affection and reverence. I knew I was very connected to Kiara, yet I didn't understand why. Effervescent happiness flooded over me every time I saw her.

I wanted to run outside and hug her tight. I felt captivated and full of *love* for Kiara.

'I am going outside!' I grabbed my outdoor gear and headed for the door. Mum and Ellette laughed.

'Yes, go and enjoy yourself!'

Gustav made his way back indoors, closing the door gently behind him.

'Kiara, you're back,' I hugged her, patting her face gently and kissing her cheek.

'Lexi, my child…'

Her voice had a soft feminine tone, which comforted me. Her large hazel eyes, with long thick lashes, peered deep into my soul— she held my gaze lovingly. It was as if we were connecting, soul to soul.

Her tall, pointy ears and soft short, antlers gave her a regal look. Such striking features and her magical presence filled my heart with love and confidence. It was a kind of majestic energy, which held a surreal quality.

I became very dreamy, yet my feet felt firmly earthed. I stood close to the magnificent deer. She seemed to be lighting up The Forest, especially for me.

It began to snow the instant I touched her smooth, velvety fur.

'Do remember, when you are back home: There is no time like the present, to have fun,' she said with a gentle, loving smile.

Rainbow coloured snowflakes appeared all around us. The snow fell steadily as The Forest danced in colours.

Kiara nudged me with her heart-shaped, shiny nose, showing me a tree stump to sit on. She brushed off the soft snow with her hoof.

'I can tell which children are kind, and which are cruel, and who deserves the wonderful opportunity like we offered you.'

'Believe what your own heart knows to be TRUE: it will always lead you to the right people, places, and truthful answers.'

Light, fluffy snowflakes flew in our direction. Kiara blew them away with one breath. Tiny gold keys dropped out of the flakes as they lay on the ground, melting.

'These golden keys resemble harmony. Throughout all your life, you will remain in perfect balance in almost all instances. Take these keys as a reminder of your time here.' Kiara placed the golden keys in a tiny bag she had around her neck, and handed it to me.

'The difficult times we go through eventually make us stronger. They are tests to see if we are ready to learn more about life on earth and ourselves,' she said.

'Then, we begin to relax and know that we are perfect, just the way we are—that everything is perfect just as it is…'

I took the bag and looked up at Kiara.

'Thank you, Kiara, for the gift of the golden keys. I know they hold your wisdom and kindness. I will always remember you.'

'You will be aware of the golden keys, but they will never attach themselves to you, or interfere with your life choices. You have been given this great GIFT: negative thoughts will no longer disturb you.'

'My dearest Lexi, remember too: it's a good thing to have feelings, they often help to guide us,' she smiled lovingly.

Kiara had dedicated her life to children and animals, so they may grow-up with love in their hearts. To love and appreciate their own unique abilities and superconscious gifts. She understood that all children are incredibly wise beings.

I hugged Kiara farewell. She turned, looked back at me, then flew up into the air, and was gone. Rainbows filled the sky as she disappeared, leaving a trail of gold dust behind.

The Forest looked so pure, so white. I was sure that today its brightness could light up the world.

I stood still, took a deep breath, held my heart and smiled. This was my moment. I knew I would remember this time *for the rest of my life…*

'Lexi…' Mum called. 'We're eating soon.' We tucked into a hearty meal: purple cauliflower and rainbow carrots, which tasted delicious. Fluffy rice and home-grown beans, foraged vegetables, with a huge bowl of sweet-potato chips, placed in the centre of the table.

The sticky-toffee-pudding was worth waiting for. It was the best part of the meal for Granddad – a perfect choice.

After an explosion of flavours, our hunger satisfied, we sat quietly together, on the comfy armchairs. No words were needed…

Mum and I left the old wooden cabin for our last sleep at the Blue Rooster Hotel. I lay in bed thinking: I was the happiest girl in the world. I was grateful for each and every moment of this adventure. I fell into a deep, deep, sleep…

What an unforgettable time.

CHAPTER 24
Secrets Revealed

THE DAY of our departure had arrived. I was sad to be leaving my new friends and this inviting place. Looking out of the hotel window at the beautiful winter wonderland for one last time felt like a dream. I could not believe everything that had happened since we arrived.

Fiddlesigh...

In London, I had been caught up in my own little world. Here, the blue skies against pristine snow was the perfect setting for an adventure.

The familiar trees, holding icicles on their branches, the iced flowers, and plants were so beautiful. I stood for a while, daydreaming.

Mum was busy closing suitcases. I needed to hug and cuddle the MAGIC CATS one last time and offer a final THANK YOU.

Leaving felt painfully *final*. There was a deep ache in my heart. I didn't want to leave—not yet.

'I'm going to miss the cats, Mum. They're my forever friends.'

'I know, darling.'

I took a final look around the room as we walked out. The lift was very slow. We decided to drag the suitcases downstairs, bouncing them, one step at a time.

'Vielen Dank!'

Mum and the hotel owner exchanged pleasantries, while someone packed the suitcases into the car.

We drove via the picturesque forest one last time. The atmosphere in the car between us was silent. Mum and I were lost in our own worlds as she drove towards Ellette's cabin.

Kiara's hoof marks were visible in the soft snow from the night before. As the car stopped, I ran off excitedly, following her tracks, while Mum went towards the front door.

'Hallo, hallo, komm,' said Gustav.

'Lexi, over here,' waved Ellette. She was standing near the bird table.

'Hello, Ellette,' I waved, and ran towards her.

Tiny, luminous bluebirds were eating from her hand.

'These birds, carry a special message for you, dear Lexi. A good attitude in life. It will travel with you when you leave here today.'

'Thank you little birds. I'm going to miss you, Ellette. The cats, the fairies, and their amazing world.

Oh! And especially Kiara—I feel her in my heart.'

'You'll be back someday. I know you will.' She smiled, and her whole body sparkled.

Small stars lit up around her head. The fairies had gathered, dressed in bright purple coats, hats, and boots. I could hear them chittering and chattering.

Belle and Trish, escorted by Ordella, waited quietly, hovering above. The twins blew me a kiss, then dropped something into my gloved hand.

'Lexi, Belle and Trish would like to present you with a gift. Go on, open it,' said Ordella, with a huge smile.

Twinkly lights appeared around us. They sparkled and shone. I opened the pretty trinket box carefully. Inside, sitting on a soft, pink velvet cushion, was a sparkling pink diamond.

'Oh! How beautiful.' I gasped. I hadn't expected such a magnificent gift.

'I will treasure it, forever.'

'If you ever feel sad, or upset, the pink diamond will light up. The pink ray will shine directly into your heart, and all will be well.'

'I love it so much!' I spun round and round, clutching the pink diamond to my chest.

'I'm so thankful.'

'Thank you for coming to say goodbye, Ordella.'

'Belle and Trish, thank you so much for this precious gift. I LOVE it!'

The twins giggled, then fluttered and flitted around my face, creating a trail of weeny stars, which circulated around my head. I was buzzing from head to toe.

The bright bluebirds and Fairy Beings waved goodbye. Soft powdery, puffs of snow began to fall as they flew away.

'See you soon, Lexi—*au revoir*,' Trish and Belle shouted in unison.

I stared with delight and disbelief at the magnificent pink diamond heart, then carefully placed the box into my coat pocket. I would keep the diamond with me always. It will forever remind me of my extraordinary adventure in The Magic Forest.

'Can we find Kiara by following her hoof prints?' I asked keenly.

'What a lovely idea, let's see where they take us.'

The hoof prints eventually led us to the where Kiara had stood the night before.

'Ellette, why can Kiara speak without eating the gold dust?' I asked curiously.

'Kiara has special powers of her own, she doesn't need the gold dust. She has already passed into the Golden Region,' she responded.

'The Golden Region? What's that?'

'That Lexi, dear cousin, is for another time…'

A small deer appeared from behind the snow-clad, Fir trees.

'Have you seen Kiara?' I asked.

'She's gone to the mountains,' said the small, spotted deer. She seemed to be in a great hurry and trotted on through the snow.

'Ellette, why would Kiara go to the mountains?'

'She meets Master Horatio and Queen Jeannie, there.'

'What do they *do* there?'

'Well, that's where they go to discuss and plan for the next generation of GOLDEN CHILDREN,' she said.

My eyes widened. 'What does *that* mean exactly?'

'The next generation of children will be born with powerful gifts. Call it a 'Universal Upgrade'. Their DNA[26] will have more strands connected, which will enhance health, lifespan and wisdom. Children won't have problems as we do now because of the upgrades.'

'*Then* what will happen?'

'The golden light is a specific frequency, a special blessing for all golden children. The way to recognise it: the child's eyes shine a very bright, gold colour.' Ellette answered.

I stood open-mouthed, and amazed, staring blankly at Ellette.

'Are you a golden-child, that's all grown up? I did see gold light in your eyes, a moment ago.'

'Yes, you did, my dear cousin,' she replied.

'I was the very first Golden-Child.'

'Do I *have* that 'special magic' in me? We *are* cousins.' I jumped up and down with excitement.

'You have released your attachments to your shyness. Now, you have to adjust to many other inner changes. You must give others time to know you, again—differently. Even dear Kitty, will need time, to accept a more confident daughter.'

'It takes time...' Ellette said, in a dreamy voice.

'Lexi, you have many questions!' I was startled by a voice from behind me.

'Ellette definitely has strong secret powers.' Queen Jeannie answered firmly. 'But, we never use our powers unwisely.'

The Queen had been around us, listening, all the while.

'Ellette is an inspiration. The first Golden-Child to appear on this sweet Earth.'

'Her parents had to sacrifice their love for her, to help all future children develop, in a completely new way. Using new methods, such as the Golden Keys and the Crystal-Star.'

With that, the Fairy Queen flew off, towards the dense forest.

'Amazing! I had no idea...'

I sighed. There was so much for me to learn, and understand.

Ellette pulled me towards her, and—arm—in—arm, we walked back to the cabin.

As we set off on the path, a herd of forest deer galloped by. They stopped abruptly, faced us, snorted gently, and trotted on. One miracle after another. How amazing life can be.

We entered the cabin in a vibrant mood. We laughed and laughed. Mum stared at us, with a knowing expression on her face. Yes, it would take her time, yet she knew this was the best kept secret between her and Ellette.

The Whistle Cabin trio had arrived to see us off: Granddad Edric , Tobias, and the hero of the mountains, Master Horatio.

Tinky, Queeny, and Ginger, were ready for hugs and fond farewells. Teddy, nowhere to be seen.

Dear TubTub was eager to say goodbye, too. He snorted and nudged his way forward. He just loved everyone. He and the cats were good friends, now.

'TubTub, wait your turn.' Granddad Edric spoke gently, not wanting to spoil our farewell.

Granddad hugged and kissed Queen Jeannie first. He knew he may not see her for a while, once she returned to her Kingdom.

I hugged Tinky warmly. Queeny placed her paws in my hand. I held the soft fluff for a few moments, as she stared into my eyes. I felt tears well up…

Ginger gave me his familiar cheek rub and hug. He was velvety soft.

Teddy appeared, he pushed and rubbed against my legs, nudging for attention. How I loved these extraordinary, MAGIC CATS!

I heard a whisper in my left ear: *'You know—I'm REALLY going to miss you.'*

'Blinky!' I jumped up and down with joy.

'Oh, Blinky, you came. Thank you!' I squealed.

'It was nothing,' she replied coyly.

'I love you ALL, so much.' Tears poured down my cheeks.

As I wiped the tears away, there was a WHOOSH—then—a SWOOP and Master Horatio landed on my shoulder.

'Goodbye my dear, Lexi.'

Horatio's big amber eyes, spoke to me with such affection. What an honour. (I must admit his landing startled me).

'Well young lady, did you enjoy your forest adventure?' Granddad laughed, with a twinkle in his eyes.

My Mum, Kitty, said her fond goodbyes too, especially to her niece, Ellette. We got into the car and I hastily opened the window. I reached out with both arms longingly...

'Bye-bye—until next time.' Gustav held my hand for a moment, then kissed me on both cheeks.

'Ve vill meet again... I know ziss...'

'OINK, OINK'...TubTub chased after the car. His piggy smile widened as he waved good-bye.

I sat back in the seat as Mum drove away. It was actually over. I felt sad, leaving all my wonderful friends behind. Tears welled up again—in Mum's eyes too. We wiped our eyes and smiled. In my heart, I knew just how much I would miss everyone.

We were almost at the airport, ready for a long flight back to London. I was downhearted, but also looking forward to going back to school. I felt more confident and had a very different attitude.

A Flight Attendant with bright red lipstick walked elegantly in her tailored uniform along the narrow aisle. Her melodic voice floating through the air:

'Tea, coffee, juice, water—anything for you, young lady?'

'Tea, with sugar and milk, please.' I replied. She smiled politely. 'What a confident young girl you are.'

I smiled. I understood perfectly. This was the NEW me. A different me. I could feel it. The Forest Fairy Team had changed me forever.

My Mum's eyes crinkled in the corners as she smiled proudly at me – her pink lipstick framing her perfectly white teeth. Afterall, it was her and Ellette that had planned this secret adventure together. I had my Mum to thank too. I squeezed her manicured hand affectionately, my heart bursting with love and gratitude.

My thoughts travelled to my take-home treasures: A pocket size quartz crystal, a pink diamond, gold keys and gold coins. Not forgetting my forever memories.

A new, exciting beginning awaits me, filled with golden opportunities. Not just for me, but for ALL children in this FUTURE Golden World.

Characters:

Ellette—Lexi's cousin
Gustav—Ellette's friend
Kitty—Lexi's mother
Lexi—main character and Kitty's daughter
Granddad Edric—Friend and neighbour
Grace—Gustav's sister
Master Horatio—wise magic Owl
Tobias—aka TubTub—special Pig friend
Kiara—wise magic Deer

The Magic Cats:

Tinky—Maitra
Teddy—Rosco
Queeny—Tilka
Ginger—Senca
Blinky
Prushka—Lexi's pet cat.

The Fairies

Belle—Fairy twin
Trish—Fairy twin
Ordella—Special Aide to the Queen
The Fairy Queen—Jeannie

Things of Interest

1. **London Heathrow**—is the biggest airport in the UK and the busiest in terms of passenger numbers. Its size covers 12.14 km². 80 million passengers per year, with only two runways.

2. **Fiddlelights**—whenever Lexi is nervous she mutters similar phrases under her breath.

3. **Thunderbirds**—a British science fiction television series using puppets. It was first shown in 1965. The series was exported to 30 countries during the 1960s.

4. **Frankfurt Airport**—is the biggest and busiest airport in Germany. It covering 23 km². 65 million passengers per year with four runways.

5. **Autobahn**—there is 8,080 miles of Autobahn, ranking it among the longest road systems in the world, with 3-4 lanes going in each direction.

6. **Witches Broomstick**—a modern Witches Broom or Besem, is made of Ash tree handles, bristles from Birch tree twigs, herbs and straw. Tied with thin strips of Willow wood. Used to purity and protect.

7. **Crystal**—most gemstones and crystals form in the Earth's crust, approximately 3 to 25 miles beneath the Earth's surface. Diamonds are buried deeper. They are part of Nature and the Earth.

8. **Phantom Crystal**—natural quartz crystals are sometimes found with rare formation inside them. These rare crystals are known for their healing properties, and the enormous energy stored in them. The rare formations have multiple 'phantoms' within the crystal.

9. **Elvish**—is the language of Elves. Similar to the Sylvan language used by the Fairies.

10. **Angeln Saddleback pig**—is a rare breed from Germany. It has large lop-ears, and is black and white in colour. It can weight as much as 300kg/600pounds.

11. **Radar**—is used for tracking and recognising objects from a distance, using radio/wi-fi waves.

12. **Bee-Sting Cake**—is a delicious Bavarian (German) vanilla dessert cake, known as 'Bienenstich Kuchen'.

13. **Monte Rosa Mountain**—is the highest mountain in the Swiss Alps. It is ±4,600 m high.

14. **Magnetic Grid**—is like electric energy that surrounds the globe/earth. The earths aura, if you like.

15. **Eagle Owl**—they have a very large wingspan and are known to have vivid orange/amber eyes. They have tufts of feathers on their heads. Eagle owls are birds of prey. They are able live in many different environments, but often build nests in rocky areas.

16. **Meditation**—is the simple training of the mind to be less busy. During meditation, you eliminate jumbled thoughts that crowd your mind and cause stress.

17. **Saluti Amice**—'greetings my friend' spoken in Latin.

18. **Hologram**—a hologram is a cross between what happens when you take a photograph, and what happens when you look at something for real. A hologram looks real and three-dimensional, and moves as you look around it, like a real object. Holograms are a bit like photographs that never dies. They're sort of 'photographic ghosts'.

19. **Rowan Tree**—since ancient times people have planted Rowan trees beside their home. In Celtic mythology it is known as the Tree of Life and symbolises courage, wisdom and protection.

20. **Portal**—a vast entrance or gateway, a huge opening.
21. **Vortex**—like swirling air or a whirlwind, a vortex spins very fast and is able to pull things into its centre. It can also be used like a doorway to another place or reality.
22. **Spells**—words spoken in a set formula, to create magic.
23. **Teleport**—going from one place to another, instantaneously.
24. **Sylvan Language**—is the language of Nature. Its speakers are often Nature Spirits, Fairies, Elves, and other Forest creatures.
25. **Tapping Energy-work**—energy flows through our bodies as well as through nature. Tapping on certain point of the body, creates a gentle balancing and healing.
26. **DNA**—contains the instructions for making a living thing. DNA provides the body with the instructions. DNA is crucial in order to live, without it we would not exist. If all the DNA in your body was put end to end, it would reach to the sun and back over 600 times.

Acknowledgements

Writing Lexi and The Magic Cats, has been a teacher and friend. Along the way there have been many inspiring people driving me forward. Firstly, my incredible cousin Celeste, without you this story would not have been written. A big hug to my young friends Alicia, Jason, Caelyn and Maryiam, thank you for reading my first draft.

Much appreciation and thanks to friends and family for your unfailing support. Especially Charmaine, Chris, Agata, Anoushka, Shendy, Caroline, Natasha, Belinda, Trish and Aggy.

To my wonderful developmental editor, Alorah Arliotis, who hit the ground running, and encouraged me to follow my dreams. Thank you to my copy editor, Keryn Delaney, she did a fantastic job. Finally, my parents, who listened and laughed as the story unfolded, day-by-day.

Attributions

I have done my utmost to find the source of the verse used in this book. I extend my apologies to anyone not credited and invite you to contact me:
roxannebarkerwriterillustrator@gmail.com

Omissions can be corrected in future editions.

About the Author

Roxanne J. Barker spent her childhood in Africa. For several years she lived and worked in Spain.

She has settled in a leafy area of S.E England and spends her time drawing, illustrating and writing. Lexi and The Magic Cats is the first of a trilogy.